For my daughter, Karin,
who journeyed across the ocean
and who inspired this story.

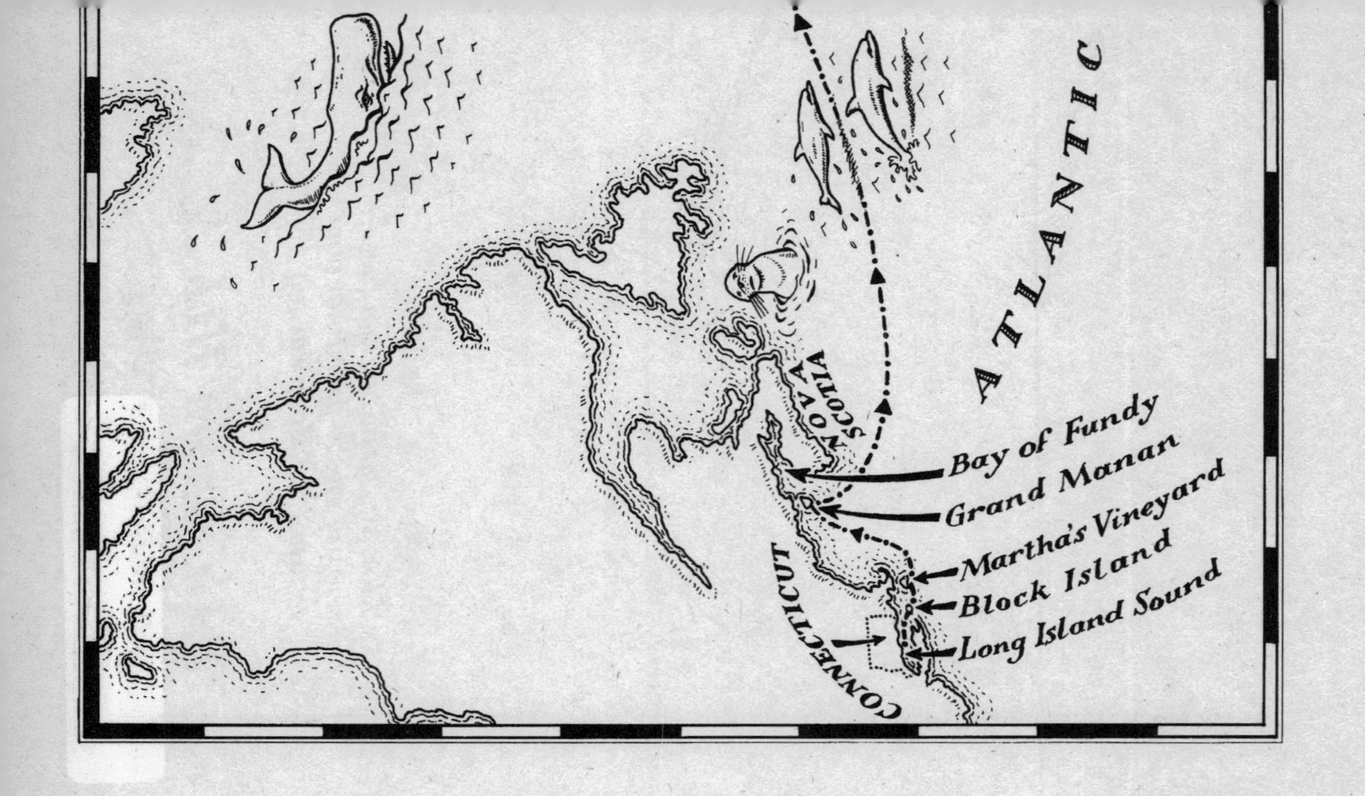
CONNECTICUT
NOVA SCOTIA
Bay of Fundy
Grand Manan
Martha's Vineyard
Block Island
Long Island Sound
ATLANTIC

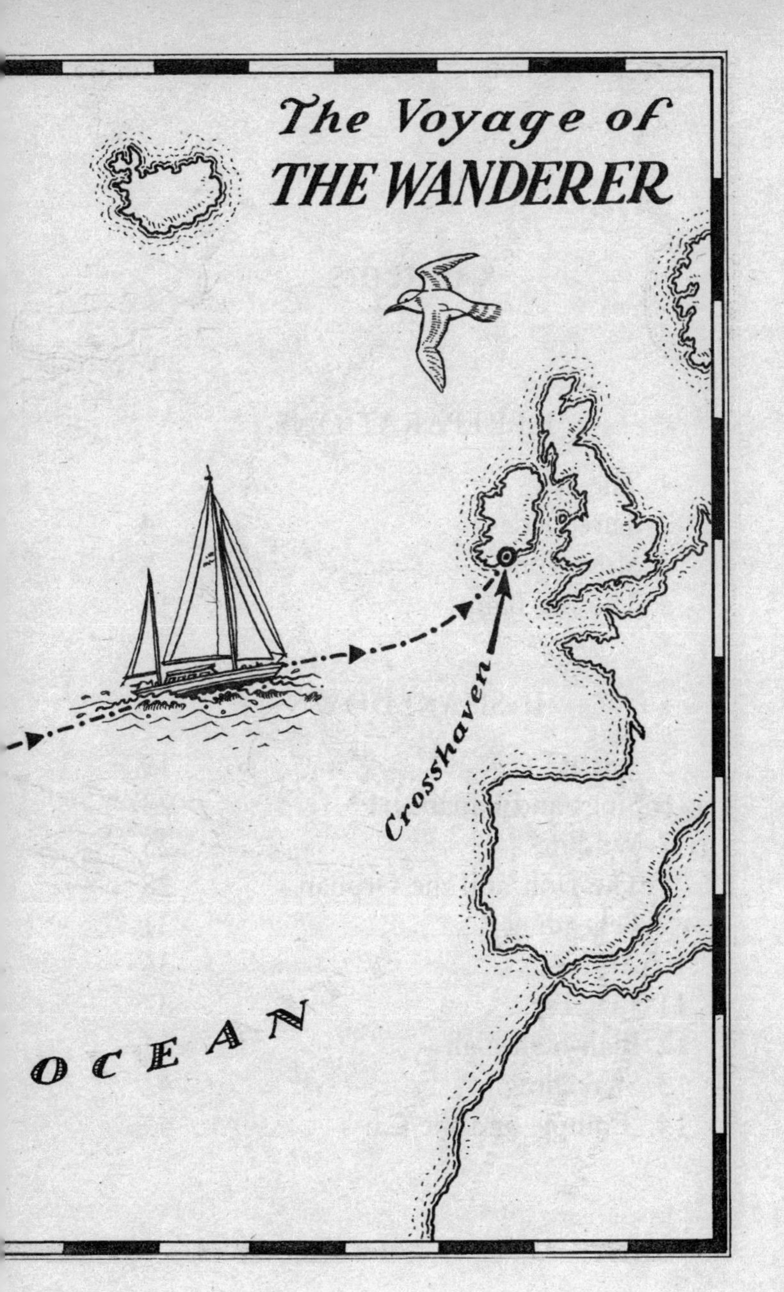
The Voyage of
THE WANDERER
Crosshaven
OCEAN

Contents

I PREPARATIONS

II SHAKEDOWN

III THE ISLAND

IV UNDER WAY

V WIND AND WAVES

VI LAND

This tale is true, and mine. It tells
How the sea took me, swept me back
And forth . . .

anonymous, *'The Seafarer'*

I

Preparations

C46364938C

1

The Sea

The sea, the sea, the sea. It rolled and rolled and called to me. *Come in*, it said, *come in.*

And in I went, floating, rolling, splashing, swimming, and the sea called, *Come out, come out*, and further I went but always it swept me back to shore.

And still the sea called, *Come out, come out,* and in boats I went – in rowboats and dinghies and motorboats, and after I learned to sail, I flew over the water, with only the sounds of the wind and the water and the birds, all of them calling, *Sail on, sail on.*

And what I wanted to do was go on and on, across the sea, alone with the water and the wind and the birds, but some said I was too young and the sea was a dangerous temptress, and at night I dreamed a terrible dream. A wall of water, towering, black, crept up behind me and hovered over me and then down, down it came, but always I awoke before the water covered me, and always I felt as if I were floating when I woke up.

2

Three Sides

I am not always such a dreamy girl, listening to the sea calling me. My father calls me Three-Sided Sophie: one side is dreamy and romantic; one is logical and down-to-earth; and the third side is hard-headed and impulsive. He says I am either in dreamland or earthland or mule-land, and if I ever get the three together, I'll be all set, though I wonder where I will be then. If I'm not in dreamland or earthland or mule-land, where will I be?

My father says my logical side is most like him, and the dreamy side most like my mother, which isn't entirely fair, I don't think. My father likes to think of himself as a logical man, but he is the one who pores over pictures of exotic lands and says things like 'We should go on a safari!' and 'We should zip through the air in a hot-air balloon!'

And although my mother is a weaver and spins silky cloths and wears flowing dresses, she is the one who gives me sailing textbooks and makes me study water safety and weather prediction and says things like, 'Yes, Sophie, I taught you to sail, but that doesn't mean I like the idea of you being out there alone on the water. I want you to stay home. Here. With me. Safe.'

My father says he doesn't know who my hard-headed mule side resembles. He says mules don't run in the family.

I am thirteen, and I am going to sail across the ocean. Although I would like to go alone – *alone! alone! flying over the water!* – I'm not. My mule-self begged a place aboard a forty-five-foot sailboat with a motley crew: three uncles and two cousins. The uncles – Stew, Mo and Dock – are my mother's brothers, and she told them, 'If the slightest harm comes to my Sophie, I'll string you all up by your toes.'

She isn't worried (although maybe she should be) about the influence of my cousin Brian – quiet, studious, serious Brian – but she frets over the bad habits I might learn from my other cousin, Cody. Cody is loud, impulsive and charming in a way my mother does not trust. 'He's *too* charming,' she says, 'in a dangerous sort of way.'

My mother isn't the only person who is not thrilled for me to take this trip. My uncles Stew and Mo tried their best to talk me out of it. 'It's going to be a bunch of us guys, doing guy things, and it wouldn't be a very pleasant place for a girl,' and 'Wouldn't you rather stay home, Sophie, where you could have a shower every day?' and 'It's a lot of hard work,' and yakkety-yak they went. But I was determined to go, and my mule-self kicked in, spouting a slew of sailing and weather terms, battering them over the head with all the things I'd learned in my sailing books and with some things I'd made up, for good measure.

Uncle Dock – the good uncle, I call him, because he's the one who doesn't see any harm in my coming – said, 'Heck, she knows more about boats than Brian and Cody put together,' and so they caved in.

There are two other reasons my mother has not tied me to my bed and refused to let me go. The first is that Uncle Dock gave her an extensive list of the safety provisions aboard the boat, which include a satellite navigator – the Global Positioning System. The second reason, not a very logical one, but one that somehow comforts my mother, is that Bompie is on the other side of the ocean. We will end up in Bompie's arms, and she wishes she could join us just for that moment.

Bompie is my grandfather – my mother's father, and also Uncles Dock, Stew and Mo's father – and he lived with my parents for many years. He is like a third parent and I love him because he is so like me. He is a man of three sides, like me, and he knows what I am thinking without my having to say it. He is a sweet man with a honey tongue and he is a teller of tales.

At the age of seventy-two, Bompie decided to go home. I thought he was already in his home, but what he meant by home was the place where he was born, and that place was 'the rolling green hills of England'.

My father was wrong about mules not running in the family. When Bompie decided to return to

England, nothing was going to stop him. He made up his mind and that was that, and off he went.

Bye-bye, Bompie.

3

Slow Time

We are hoping to set sail the first week of June, right after school ends. These final weeks are limping by, plodding hour after plodding hour. In my head, though, I am hurling myself towards that final day, picturing every little detail of it. I told my parents that I would zip home on the last day of school, grab a backpack, snare a ride to the bus station and meet my uncles and cousins in Connecticut, and off we would all go, sailing out into the sea.

'Not so fast, Sophie,' my father said. 'When the time comes, your mother and I will drive you there. We're not dumping you on a bus by yourself.'

Alas. In the wee little town where we live, everyone is having adventures except me. We used to live on the coast of Virginia, curling up against the ocean, but last year my parents came up with their Great Plan to move us to the countryside, because my mother was missing the Kentucky mountains where she'd grown up. So we moved to this sleepy town, where the only water is the Ohio River, which is as sleepy as the town. People here sure love that river, but I don't know why. It doesn't have waves or tides. There are no crabs or jellyfish living in it. You can't even see very much of it at a time, only a little stretch up to the next bend.

But for kids in my class, that river is like paradise, and they have had adventures on it and off it. They have fished in that river, swum in it, rafted down it. I want to do things like that, but I want to do them on the sea, out on the wide, wide ocean.

When I told some of my friends that I was going to sail across the ocean, one said, 'But it's nice here, with the river rolling along every single day.'

Another said, 'But you just got here. We don't know anything about you. Like where you lived before, and—'

I didn't want to get into all that. I wanted to start from zero. That had been one good thing about moving here. It had been like starting over.

Another said, 'Why would you want to be a prisoner on a boat anyway?'

'Prisoner?' I said. 'Prisoner? I'll be as free as that little jaybird up there floating in the sky!'

And so I told them about the waves calling me and the rolling sea and the open sky, and when I finished, they pretty much yawned and said, 'What-ev-er,' and 'You could die out there,' and 'If you don't come back, can I have that red jacket of yours?' I figured they were probably never going to accept my adventure, and I was just going to have to go without their understanding why I wanted to go.

My mother gave me this journal I'm writing in. She said, 'Start now. Write it down. All of it. And when you come back, we can read it, and it'll be as if we were there too.'

My teachers don't want to hear about it, though.

'Sophie! Put away that sailing book and get out your math book!'

'Sophie! School isn't over yet! Knuckle down to business! Get out that grammar homework!'

Yesterday, Uncle Dock phoned and said that we won't be setting out across the ocean as soon as I get there. There is work to be done first, 'a lot, a lot of work!'

I don't mind the thought of work because I like to mess around with boats, but I want to get out on that ocean so bad I can feel it and taste it and smell it.

4

The Big Baby

In the end, it was only my father who drove me to Connecticut. My mother said she could not guarantee that she'd behave like an adult. She was afraid she would 'dissolve into a blob of jelly' and cling to me and not let me go. I kept telling her that this was just a little trip across the ocean, no big deal. We're not even sailing the boat back because Uncle Dock is leaving it with a friend in England.

I think my mother imagines horrible things happening on that ocean, but she will not say so aloud. My own mind does not want to imagine horrible things.

'Sometimes,' my father said, 'there are things you just have to do. I think this might be one of those things for Sophie.' That surprised me. It did feel as if it was something I *had* to do, but I couldn't have said why, and I was surprised and grateful that my father understood this without my having to explain it.

'OK, OK, OK!' my mother said. 'Go! And you'd better come back home in one piece!'

For two long weeks, my uncles and cousins and I have been holed up together in Uncle Dock's small cottage. I am beginning to think we'll never live through this time on land, let alone the sea journey. We'll probably kill each other first.

The boat is propped up on dry land and was a sorry sight the first day, I have to admit. It didn't look anywhere near ready to head out to sea. But it has a terrific name: *The Wanderer.* I can picture myself on this sailboat, wandering out across the sea, wandering, wandering.

The boat belongs to Uncle Dock, and he calls it his 'baby'. It seems huge to me, enormous, far, far bigger than any boat I've ever been on. It's forty-five feet long (that's a pretty big 'baby'), navy and white, with two masts of equal size and nifty booms that wrap around the sails.

Below deck there's sleeping for six (four in the forward section, two in the back); a galley with icebox, sink and stove; a table (two of the beds double as bench-seats for the table); a bathroom; a chart table and navigation equipment; and cubby-holes and closets.

Uncle Dock, who is a carpenter in his real life, walked us around *The Wanderer* the first day, pointing out things that needed fixing. 'This baby needs a little attention,' he said. 'Rudder needs work, yep, and the keel too, yep,' and 'That whole bilge needs redoing, yep,' and 'Those electrics – gotta rewire, yep,' and 'Whole thing needs sprucing up, yep.'

Yep, yep, yep.

My cousin Brian was busy making a list of all these things on his clipboard. 'Right, then!' Brian said, after we'd walked around and around the boat.

'Here's the list. I figure we should also make a list of the equipment we'll need—'

His father, Uncle Stew, interrupted. 'That's my boy, a real organizer!'

Uncle Stew's real name is Stuart, but everyone calls him Stew because he worries and stews about every little tiny weeny thing. He is tall and thin, with a scrub of black hair on his head. Uncle Stew's son, Brian, looks like a younger photocopy of him. They both walk in a clumsy, jerky sort of way, as if they are string puppets, and they both place a high value on being organized.

While Brian was still making up his list, my other cousin, Cody, started fiddling with the rudder. 'Not yet!' Uncle Stew said. 'We're not organized yet!'

Brian said, 'We'll get all our lists together and then divide up the jobs.'

'That's my boy,' Uncle Stew said, 'a real take-charge sort of guy.'

Yep.

It's hot, ninety-five degrees most days, and everyone has his own idea about how things should be fixed. Uncle Mo spends a lot of time leaning back in a deckchair, watching the rest of us and barking orders: 'Not that way – start on the other side!' and 'You knuckleheaded doofus! Is that any way to use a brush?' Mostly this is aimed at his son, Cody, who has selective deafness. Cody can hear the rest of us just fine, but he can't ever seem to hear his father.

Uncle Mo is a bit on the chubby side, and he likes lounging around with his shirt off, getting a tan. His son, Cody (the one my mother thinks is charming in a dangerous sort of way), however, is fit and muscular, always humming or singing, and smiling that wide, white smile of his. Girls who stroll through the boatyard on their way to the public beach stop and watch him, hoping to catch his attention.

And Uncle Dock is easygoing and calm. Nothing seems to faze him, not all the work that needs doing, or the mishaps that occur – like when Brian knocked over a can of varnish, or when Cody gouged the deck or when Uncle Stew tangled the lines. Uncle Dock shrugs and says, 'We'll just fix it, yep.'

On the second day, after Uncle Stew and Brian had doled out most of the assignments to everyone else, I said, 'What about me? What do you want me to do?'

'You?' Uncle Stew said. 'Oh. Yeah. I guess you could clean up – you know, scrub things out.'

'I want to fix something.'

Uncle Stew laughed a fake laugh. 'Huh, huh, huh. And what do you think you could fix, Sophie? Huh, huh, huh.'

'I'd like to do that bilge—'

'Oh?' he said, smiling all around at everyone else, as if they were sharing a private joke. 'Now, how exactly might you do that?'

And so I told him how it could be redesigned and what sort of equipment I might need, and the more

I talked, the more Uncle Stew's smile faded, and wider grew the grin on Uncle Dock's face.

'See?' Uncle Dock said. 'She knows something about boats. Let her tackle the bilge.'

Brian, with his clipboard in hand, jerked his puppet-arm and said, 'Who's going to do the cleaning, then? I don't have anyone down for cleaning—'

'We'll all clean,' Uncle Dock said.

'Not me,' Uncle Mo said, 'I'm a lousy cleaner. Ask anybody.'

And so we (all of us except Uncle Mo, who was lying in his chair getting a tan) have spent these hot, sweaty days working on *The Wanderer* at the marina. We've repaired the rudder and keel, redesigned the bilge, rewired the electrics and organized and cleaned.

This morning *The Wanderer* came off her cradle. Dock and Brian and I were on board as the crane lifted *The Wanderer* up in a sling and lowered her into the water. It was such an eerie feeling: down, down, down she went. I didn't think it was going to stop going down, but then there was a *floop* and a wobble and there she was, bobbing like a cork.

Afloat!

'You OK, Brian?' Dock asked. 'You look a little wobbly.'

'Sort of want to throw up,' Brian said. 'This boat looks awful small now in the water. This is all that will keep us alive?'

'Small?' Uncle Dock said. 'This here *Wanderer* is a pretty big baby.'

'Our little island home,' I said.

I sent a postcard to my parents. I told them that soon I was going wandering on *The Wanderer*.

II

Shakedown

5

Afloat

We have begun!

Last night, when we sailed by the stars along the Connecticut coastline on a trial run, I thought my heart would leap out into the sky. Overhead, all was velvety blue-black pierced with pearly stars and blending into shimmery black ocean. The smell of the sea, the feel of the wind on your face and your arms, the flapping of the sails – oh, it was magic!

We are really on the way! The sea is calling, calling, *Sail on, sail on!* and the gentle rocking of *The Wanderer* makes me think of Bompie – was it Bompie? – holding me on his lap when I was young, whispering stories into the air.

The first leg of our journey will take us through Long Island Sound to Block Island, and then a short hop on to Martha's Vineyard, a loop around Cape Cod and up the northern coast, and then on to Nova Scotia, and finally the long stretch to Ireland and to England – land of Bompie! Uncle Dock estimates that it will take us three to four weeks, depending on how long we stop when we spy land.

Cody is keeping a journal too, only he calls it a

dog. When I first heard him say that, I said, 'You mean a *log*?'

He said, 'No, a dog. A dog-log.' He said he is keeping this dog-log because he has to, for a summer project. 'It was either that or read five books,' he said. 'I figure it'll be a lot easier keeping a dog-log than reading all those words somebody else wrote.'

Uncle Dock maintains the official captain's log, and in the front of it are neat maps that chart our journey. Uncle Stew and Brian said they'd be too busy 'to record the highlights', and when I asked Uncle Mo if he was going to keep any sort of record of the trip, he yawned. 'Oh,' he said, tapping his head, 'I'll keep it all in here. And maybe I'll sketch a few things.'

'You mean draw? You can draw?'

'Don't sound so surprised,' he said.

I *was* surprised, because it doesn't seem like he has the energy to do much of anything.

We all have daily chores (from Brian's list) and duty watches, and Uncle Stew came up with the idea that each of us has to teach something along the way.

'Like what?' Cody asked.

'Anything – navigating by instruments, by stars—'

'Right,' Cody said. 'Easy for you, but what if we don't know any of that stuff?'

'You must know something you could teach us,' Uncle Stew said with a little smirk.

'How about juggling?' Cody said. 'I could teach you all how to juggle.'

'Juggle?' Brian said.

'Doofus,' Cody's father said.

'I'd like to learn how to juggle,' I said. 'I bet it's not as easy as it looks.'

'What's juggling got to do with anything?' Brian asked.

'Well, if you think it'd be too hard for you—' Cody said.

'Who said anything about hard? I could juggle. It just seems a stupid thing to learn on a boat.'

I'm not sure yet what I could teach, but I'll think of something. We have to decide by tonight.

The weather is perfect today – sunny and warm – the current is with us, and the wind has been gently nudging us towards the hazy cliffs of Block Island. I've been to Block Island before, once, but I don't remember who it was with. My parents and grandfather? I remember walking on top of a big hill with lush purple and yellow flowers and scraggly brush growing around the rocks. And I remember the old blue pickup truck with lawn chairs in the back and riding along narrow lanes, staring out at the ocean and singing, 'Oh, here we are on the Island of Block, in a big blue pickup truuuuuck—'

My grandfather bought me a captain's cap, which I wore every day. We went clamming at night, and I scouted aeroplanes in the cottage loft.

And every summer after that, I longed to return to Block Island, but we never did. There wasn't time.

I've thought of something I could teach my boat family: the stories that Bompie taught me.

*

Dock and Cody have just caught two bluefish. Success! But I didn't like watching Cody club and gut them. We're all going to have to do this, though. It's one of the rules. It's my turn next, and I don't want to do it.

But the bluffs of Block Island are in sight, and the bluefish is filleted for lunch, and I am hungry . . .

6

Slugs and Bananas

Cody's log . . .

My father is driving me bananas. He lies around like a slug and doesn't help with anything and barks orders right and left. Sophie is lucky; she doesn't have any parents to bug her.

Uncle Stew said the only reason she's on this trip is because Uncle Dock took pity on the orphan. That's what Uncle Stew calls Sophie: the orphan. I want to slug him when he calls her that.

Sophie talks about my aunt and uncle as if they are her real parents, even though they are only her adopted parents and she's only been with them three years. Brian says Sophie lives in a dream world, but I think it's kind of neat that she does that. At least she isn't sitting around moping about being an orphan.

Sometimes I wish I were an orphan, because my father is a big crab and my mother is afraid of him and always hiding in the corner looking pitiful.

But I guess I'm not supposed to write about stuff like that in this dog-log. I guess I'm supposed to write about the journey and all that.

We started it. The journey, I mean. Amazing. I thought we were going to be stuck on land forever, what with Brian coming up with new lists every day. That boy sure likes to make lists. So does his father. They're a real list-making team.

Nothing is happening except that the boat is actually sailing and not leaking too much or tipping over. Yet.

7

Wildlife

Last night, after anchoring *The Wanderer* in the Block Island harbour, Cody and Brian and I took the dinghy to land and walked along the beach. Brian can be a real fusspot, carefully rolling up his jeans so they won't get wet, and leaping out of the way of the waves, and constantly checking his watch.

'It's seven ten,' he announced, and then ten minutes later, 'It's seven twenty,' and then ten minutes later, 'It's seven thirty.'

'Give it a rest, OK?' Cody said. 'What does it matter what time it is?'

Brian dodged a rock wedged in the sand and jumped back from the ocean spray breaking around it. 'We have to be back before dark,' he said.

Cody looked at the sun, hovering in the western sky. 'You know what? I bet we'll be able to tell when it's starting to get dark – without a watch!'

'Huh, huh, huh,' Brian said.

Two girls were coming from the opposite direction. 'Hey, look, some wildlife!' Cody said to Brian.

'Where? What?'

'The babes,' Cody said, eyeing the girls. 'The babes.'

One of the wildlife babes stopped in front of Cody and smiled sweetly at him. 'Hey,' she said.

'Hey,' Cody said.

'You wouldn't, like, you know, happen to know what time it is, would you?' she asked. Her friend blushed and flicked something off her arm.

'Huh, huh, huh,' Brian said, jerking his puppet-arm, and dangling his watch-laden wrist in front of Cody. 'Sometimes a watch comes in handy,' Brian said.

We returned to *The Wanderer* (before dark, much to Brian's relief) and spent the night on board in the harbour instead of sailing on, because Uncle Dock said we need to do some more fine-tuning.

Today, more sun!

I went up the mast in the bosun's chair for the first time, to replace the bulb for the anchor light. Up there, you can see for miles and miles, to the ends of Block Island and across the ocean: water and more water and sky and more sky. And since there are no stays on these masts, you really feel the motion of the boat and the water up there. You feel the air on your face and in your hair, you smell the sea, you feel so free.

Later, while Uncle Dock was tinkering with the electrics, Cody and I returned to shore and walked down the beach to the lighthouse and on back to the bird sanctuary. Cody spotted a fuzzy chick and said, 'Hey, you little chick. Hey, you fuzzball,' which surprised me, because usually he is busy flexing his muscles and you wouldn't expect him to be so tender with little birds. As we left, he called, 'Bye-bye, birdies.'

He sure is a funny kind of guy. One minute he is talking about babes and the next minute he is talking to the birdies.

We are barely under way with our journey, and already everything seems more fluid and relaxed. I wear what is dry and near. I go to sleep right before I collapse, and wake up to the sound of people talking in the cockpit. I'm ready to get out on the open ocean, though. I want to be moving, to be sailing, where it doesn't matter if it's day or night, where time is all connected. I'd like to catch a fish, to feed myself directly from the ocean. I hope to be a voyager, a wanderer, sailing on to Bompie!

8

The Dolt and the Orphan

Had to get away from Dad last night, so I went with Sophie and Brian over to the island. Brian's getting on my nerves. First he had to ask a zillion questions like was he wearing the right clothes and should he take a jacket, and then the next minute he was telling us how to paddle and how to tie up the dinghy and all that jazz. Next thing he's going to be telling me is how to breathe.

Brian gets on Sophie's case too. She said something about how her mother wouldn't like hearing me call girls 'wildlife' or 'babes', and Brian stopped in his tracks and said her mother wasn't here, so tough beans. Then, to rub it in more, he added, 'And which mother are you talking about, anyway?'

Sophie didn't miss a beat. She picked up a rock and sailed it out across the water. 'Look at that!' she said. 'Can you throw that far?' I couldn't tell whether she hadn't heard him or whether she was ignoring him.

I told him to shut his yap. He said, 'I don't have to if I don't want to.' What a dolt.

Today Sophie and I escaped without Brian and went back to the island. Sophie's a lot easier to be around than anyone else on the boat. She's always taking deep breaths and smiling at the wind and the sun and the waves. She doesn't get on your case about stuff.

I almost put my foot in it though. We found one little chick stumbling along by itself in the brush and I said, 'Hey, it's an orphan!'

Sophie said, 'It is not!' and she scooped it up and took it back to a nest we'd seen.

I wish I hadn't said the thing about the orphan.

Sophie also went up in the bosun's chair today. Uncle Dock had been standing around staring up at the light thingy at the top of the mast, wondering how we were going to change it.

'Want me to go up there?' Sophie asked.

'Maybe Brian ought to do it,' he said. 'Brian? Go up in that bosun's chair and change that thing, OK?'

'No way!' Brian said. He looked green. That mast is a tall, tall spire.

'Cody! How about you?'

'I don't think so,' I said. OK, so I wasn't thrilled about it. I don't much like heights.

Sophie said, 'Listen! I'm the lightest and the smallest. It makes sense for me to go. I'd *love* to go!'

'I just don't want you getting hurt, that's all,' Uncle Dock said.

I guess that meant he didn't mind if Brian or I got hurt. Geez.

Sophie said, 'Hey! Are you going to treat me like that the whole trip? Aren't you going to let me do *anything*?'

So Uncle Dock reluctantly let her go up, and you should have seen her! She was laughing and shouting 'Whoopeeee!' She scurried up there in no time, and got that bulb changed and said, 'Let me swing up here a bit, OK? It's brilliant up here!'

'She'd better not get hurt up there,' Uncle Dock said.

Last night we all had to say what we were going to teach everyone else on our voyage. That's one of Uncle Stew's big ideas. Uncle Dock is teaching us how to read charts, Brian is teaching points of sail (whatever that is), Uncle Stew is teaching us how to use the sextant thingy, my dad is teaching us radio code or something like that and I'm teaching juggling. That really ticked some of them off, that I was teaching something 'dumb' like juggling. But I don't care. Juggling is cool.

It got a little weird when Sophie said what she was teaching. She said she was going to teach us Bompie's stories.

'And how do you know Bompie's stories?' Brian asked.

''Cause he told them to me.'

Nobody said a word.

Later, Brian said to me, 'What the heck is she talking about? She's never even met Bompie!'

'Leave her alone,' I said.

9

Beheading

We left Block Island early to begin what was expected to be a sixteen-hour sail. Everyone was on deck as we set off for Martha's Vineyard.

'Ahoy! Blast off!' Cody shouted into the wind. Cody likes to annoy his father by mixing sailing terminology with whatever flies into his mind, and he often gets the sailing terms wrong, or uses them at the wrong time or uses them all together. 'Reef the rudder and heave ho, take off!' You can see Uncle Mo grinding his teeth whenever Cody does this. Brian and Uncle Stew don't find Cody funny, either, but Uncle Dock doesn't seem to mind, and I like it. It makes me feel less self-conscious about getting everything right.

'Winch the mast and hoist the boom!' Cody shouted.

'Cut it out,' Brian said. 'You might have to get it right sometime when our lives count on it, and either you won't know what to say or no one will listen because you talk gibberish all the time.'

'Aw, lighten up, Brian,' Cody said. 'Reef your sails.'

The wind and current were with us all day, and

so were the fish. We caught seven bluefish, but two got away. I killed (*killed!*), beheaded (*beheaded!*) and gutted (*gutted!*) the first two, with Uncle Stew and Brian standing over me. You could tell they were hoping I'd chicken out or that I'd make a mess of it.

'Bludgeon it first,' Uncle Stew instructed. 'Between the eyes.'

'Hit it with the winch handle,' Brian said.

'Beat the wench!' Cody said.

'Not the *wench*, you idiot,' Brian said. 'The *winch*. And she's not beating the winch, she's beating the fish *with* the winch.'

'Light-en up, man, light-en up!' Cody said.

With the winch handle, I bludgeoned the poor, helpless, defenceless fish.

'The idea,' Brian said, 'is to kill them as quickly as possible.'

Beating that poor fish really bothered me. I kept telling myself that I'd been eating meat and fish all my life and I'd never thought twice about it.

'You think it's dead?' I asked.

'No,' Brian said. 'Cut off its head.'

'Execute it!' Cody said. 'Off with your head!'

I got the fish's head cut halfway off and I was thinking, *OK, Sophie, OK, it won't feel this* – and then as soon as I started in on the other side, the fish started flipping and floundering.

'Get on with it,' Uncle Stew said.

'Yeah, hurry up,' Brian added.

The hardest part, I learned, is not the beating, not the blood, not the guts, not the slitting the throat.

The hardest part is breaking the spine. That part makes my heart skip, flip, wobble. When my fingers fold around the spine – that power line – and turn the head to the left or right, I feel a massive release of something – pressure, tension, energy, or maybe just pure life force – in the two or three seconds that it takes to break the spine. Where does that force go?

We made great time today, pulling into Vineyard Haven on Martha's Vineyard within eight hours – half our expected time.

'We are voyagers!' I shouted when we spotted land.

'Land ho, avast and abast and aghast!' Cody shouted.

The main reason we were stopping here was to visit Uncle Dock's friend Joey, who'd spent the last five years rebuilding an old wooden boat that he'd found in a swamp. Joey's boat is immaculate, with an all-teak interior and exterior, a sleek design.

I kept running my hands over that beautiful wood until Uncle Dock said, 'Well, she's a beauty, but *The Wanderer* is still my love.' I think he was a little jealous because of the fuss I was making over Joey's boat.

'I think *The Wanderer* is a beauty too, Dock,' I said. 'And if I had to choose which one to sail across the ocean, I'd choose *The Wanderer.*'

'Yep,' he said. 'Me too.'

Joey invited us to his cottage for dinner. It seemed

weird being in a house. So much wasted space! You could fit so much stuff in there! On the boat there is a place for everything, and everything is compact and small, and nothing is on board that isn't needed. There's no room for extra junk.

After dinner, Cody and I were sitting on the dock when Brian came out and said, 'Something's up.'

'What do you mean?' Cody asked.

Brian kicked at the dock. 'Dock and Joey were in the kitchen talking, and I just went in to get some water, and they shut up so fast. Do you think they were talking about me?'

'Don't flatter yourself,' Cody said.

'Well, then, what were they talking about? What's the big secret?'

'How should I know?' Cody said.

'Sometimes people need their own secrets,' I said.

'You oughta know,' Brian said.

Brian is like a woodpecker, peck-peck-pecking away. I was glad to get back to the boat and take my sleeping bag up on deck and sit down with my log.

Uncle Stew has been taking his sleeping bag out on the dock.

'What's the matter?' Cody asked him. 'You feeling seasick?'

'I never get seasick,' Uncle Stew barked. 'I just like to sleep on the dock.'

'Yeah, right,' Cody said.

*

I'm going to stop writing soon and then I'll fall asleep with the stars overhead and the clinking of lines against masts in the harbour. I love the way the boat rocks you to sleep like a baby.

10

Ahoy

Ahoy! I could get into this sailing stuff. We're whipping along! Man! And I don't have to be on watch with my dad, so that's cool. Nobody to bug me except Brian, but he's easier to ignore than my dad.

Sophie is a riot catching fish. I've never seen anyone so happy about something so simple. I thought she was going to puke, though, when she had to kill the first one. She kept saying, 'It's still alive! It's in pain! It's hurting!' Then when my dad got the fish cooked, Sophie said she wasn't hungry.

My dad is on my case big-time. He's trying to talk me out of doing the juggling thing.

He said, 'Don't you know anything else you could teach?'

I said, 'Nope.'

11

Juggling

More work on *The Wanderer* today. I finished off Buddy the Bilge Box, the fibreglass wonder, coating it with resin to plug any minor leaks.

Uncle Dock said, 'You did a fine job on Buddy the Bilge, yep.' I was hoping he'd point that out to the others, but instead he said, 'I guess we'd better get moving. Too much boat attitude here anyway.'

'How so?' I asked.

'You know: *my boat is better than your boat*, and *my boat is bigger than your boat*, and all that. Boat attitude.'

I think he's a little sensitive about the state of *The Wanderer*. I hadn't really noticed how strange our boat might look until I saw all the sleek boats in the harbour here. They're gleaming! People dressed in spiffy matching clothes are on deck polishing everything in sight. You don't see a thing out of place.

The Wanderer, though, is splotched with caulk, including white footprints across the deck from where someone had stepped in it; our clothes are hanging off the lines in hopes of drying; pots and pans are piled on the deck because Cody and I brought them up top to scrub; and we're wearing our normal grubby shorts and T-shirts and bandannas.

'Time to move on,' Dock grumbled.

'Ahoy then!' Cody said. 'Boom the anchor!'

Uncle Mo was lounging on the deck. 'Cody,' he said, 'knock it off.'

'Knock off the anchor!' Cody said.

'Go help Brian with the charts,' Uncle Mo said. 'Make yourself useful.'

Cody leaped off the side into the water. 'Man overboard! Glug, glug, glug.'

It's hard not to laugh at Cody, but I do sometimes wonder if he has any brains in his head or if he ever thinks any serious things, and I'm beginning to see how it might get kind of annoying to be holed up with him for three whole weeks on this little island of a boat.

Today Brian tried to teach us points of sail. Most of us already knew all that, but if we hadn't already known it, we sure wouldn't have learned it from Brian. He launched into a complicated explanation of how the wind relates to the sail and the boat's direction.

'So when the wind is from ahead,' Brian lectured, 'that's called *beating*—'

'Beating? Like this you mean?' Cody beat his chest.

Brian ignored him. 'And when the wind is from the side, that's called *reaching*—'

'Reaching? Like this?' Cody reached out way over the rail as if he were stretching for something.

'Knock it off, Cody. And when the wind is from astern—'

'What's astern?' Cody asked.

'Don't you even know *that*?' Brian shouted. 'Astern is back there – the back of the boat. If you're not going to take this seriously—' he warned.

'I don't see why we have to know all those terms. I mean, so what if we don't know a *beat* from a *reach*? You only have to know how to *do* it, right? Not what to call it.'

Brian said, 'Do you really know how to *do* any of this? Do you know where the wind is coming from and what to do with the sails if it's coming from, say, behind us?'

'What do I have to know that for?' Cody said. 'Everybody else seems to know and everybody's always barking orders, so I just do what people tell me to do. I can haul in a line as good as anyone.'

'Huh,' Brian said.

Later, we got our first juggling lesson from Cody. I thought he was a really good teacher because he started out very simply, with just one thing to toss in the air. We were practising with packets of pretzels.

'This is stupid,' Brian said.

Uncle Mo was on watch, but he turned around to mutter, 'Juggling. Geez.'

Then Cody had us toss two pretzel packets in the air, one from each hand. That was easy too. But when we added the third pretzel packet, we were all fumbling and clumsy. Pretzels went zinging over the side of the boat.

'It's all in the motion of your hands,' Cody said. 'Just get in a rhythm.'

'This is really stupid,' Brian said.

'It might help your coordination,' Cody said.

'What's wrong with my coordination?'

It got ugly after that, so we stopped the juggling lesson.

Brian and Uncle Dock are going over the charts and trying to catch the weather forecast on the radio. Tomorrow we leave for Nova Scotia, a straight ocean sail that should take three or four days, with no sight of land. *No land!* I can't imagine it; I can't think what it will be like to see nothing but ocean, ocean all around.

'This will be our first big shakedown, yep,' Uncle Dock said.

Uncle Stew tapped his fingers on the table. 'Weather forecast doesn't sound too good.'

'Aw, what's a little weather?' Uncle Mo said.

12

Blah-blah-blah

Stupid day.

Stupid Brian was blah-blah-blahing about points of sail, as if he knows everything there is to know about everything.

He doesn't know how to juggle, that's for sure.

This morning, Brian said to me, 'You like Sophie better than me, don't you?'

I said, 'Yep.'

Well. It's the truth.

Tomorrow Sophie is going to tell the first of Bompie's stories. Now, *that* ought to be interesting.

13

Shakedown

I'm not really sure what day it is any more. These duty watches are warping my sense of time.

For the first couple of days, there were two of us on a watch (I was paired with Uncle Dock), and we were on for four hours at a time, off for eight, then on for four more. Four hours is a lot, especially when it's dark, and every muscle in your body is tensed, listening, watching. Everyone else is asleep then and you know it's only the two of you keeping them safe.

Out here, there isn't day and night and then a new day. Instead, there are degrees of light and dark, merging and changing. It's like one long stream of time unfolding in front of you, all around you. There isn't really a *yesterday* or a *day before*, which is weird, because then what is *tomorrow*? And what is *last week* or *last year*? And if there is no yesterday or last year – or ten years ago – then it must be all *now*, one huge big present thing.

This makes me feel very strange, as if I could say, 'Now I am four,' and by saying so, I could be four again. But that can't be. Not really. Can it?

We've been sailing up through the Gulf of Maine,

towards Grand Manan Island in the Bay of Fundy, just west of Nova Scotia. Uncle Dock calls the wind 'a capricious lady' because it comes in fits and starts. Yesterday (I still have to use words like *yesterday*, because I don't know how else to talk about things that happened *before*), when we had a spell of fog, Uncle Dock recited a poem about fog creeping along on little cat feet, and as soon as he said that, that's what I saw when I looked out into the grey mist: hundreds of little cat feet tiptoeing along. Later, when the fog rolled along in deeper, darker clumps, I imagined great big tiger feet loping towards us – soft, furry, graceful tiger feet.

I had a mournful lonely spell when I was on watch, peering through all that grey, and suddenly I didn't want to leave the shores of North America, to set off across the ocean, to be so far from land. But I didn't have long to be mournful, because the wind came up strong from the north, which meant we had to do a lot of tacking and heeling. The waves were huge – six to eight feet – or at least I thought they were huge, but Uncle Stew called them baby waves.

'You getting scared, Sophie?' Uncle Stew said, and it seemed as if he hoped I *was* scared, so I said, 'No, I'm not a bit scared. Not the least bit.' I *was* scared, but I didn't want him to know it.

Below deck, it was chaos. It was Cody's and my turn to cook lunch, and we had food sloshed all over the place.

'Mind the mizzen pot! Hoist the flibbergibbet!'

Cody shouted, as the pot's hot contents went sloshing over the side.

'Cody, are you *ever* serious?' I said.

He tossed a clamshell right in the soup. 'Oh brother,' he said, 'sooner or later, everybody asks me that.'

I guess it's a touchy subject.

The Wanderer has had a few problems on her first shakedown: leaks in the aft cabin and water in the sump. We spend a lot of time crawling around looking for trouble and then trying to fix whatever's wrong. So far we've been able to plug all the leaks. You don't feel too worried when you know you can get to land within an hour or two if you have to, or where there is enough boat traffic so that you can hail help easily, but once we set off from Nova Scotia, what will we do if we spring a major leak?

I don't want to think about that. I'd rather think about the good omens: dolphins have visited us three times! They come in groups of four or five and swim alongside the boat. They usually come when we're sailing fast, whipping along. It's as if they're racing us. They play up in front of the bow, darting back and forth right below the water, only inches from the hull.

They're the most graceful creatures I've ever seen, gliding through the water without any apparent effort, and then arching at the surface and raising their fins and backs out of the water.

Cody calls them *darlings*. 'Here, dolphin darlings! Over here!'

I always feel a little sad when they finally swim away and Cody calls, 'Bye-bye, dolphin darlings! Bye-bye!'

We've changed the shifts around in order to have three people on watch through the fog (Cody's on with us now). Right now I'm bundled up in my foul-weather gear, watching the sun rise in front of us and the moon set at our stern. I'm tired and damp and desperately need a shower, but I am in heaven.

I'm learning so much every day, and the more I learn, the more I realize how much more there is to know about sailing and water and navigation and weather. Today Uncle Stew gave us a lesson in sextant readings. It's harder than I expected, and Uncle Stew and Brian keep scolding me and Cody, telling us we're not pulling our weight unless we learn how to do all this, because their lives might depend on the two of us.

'You'd better *hop*e your lives don't depend on me and Sophie,' Cody joked.

Uncle Stew got mad. 'Not everything is funny, Cody, and when you're in the middle of that ocean, you'll be praying that if anything happens, everybody on board this boat will be capable of saving your hide. You could at least do the same for us.'

'Yeah, yeah, yeah, I hear ya,' Cody said, as he went below deck.

Even Uncle Dock seemed annoyed at Cody this time. 'I sure hope that boy gets serious about something,' he said.

*

I had a dream last night (or was it in the afternoon? or the morning? or the day before?) about being adrift in the ocean with no food, and we were all languishing on deck with no energy to do anything, and the boat was tossing and heaving around, and then a seagull flew overhead and landed on the boom and Brian said, 'Kill it! Kill it!'

It's now about two in the afternoon, and the sun has broken through the clouds, and we're about thirty-six miles from Grand Manan. We're hoping to get there before dark. It's my watch now, so I'd better get busy.

14

Bompie and the Car

Today I heard Brian ask Uncle Stew what happened to Sophie's real parents.

Uncle Stew said, 'No idea.'

'How come you don't know?' Brian asked.

Uncle Stew shrugged. 'Nobody ever tells me anything.'

So I asked my father what happened to Sophie's real parents, and he said, 'I'll tell you someday.'

'Tell me now.'

'No, don't think so.'

Got yelled at for not understanding all the navigation gobbledygook. Got yelled at for joking around too much. Got yelled at for breathing. Well, almost.

Sophie told her first Bompie story today. It went something like this:

When Bompie was a young man, he lived on a farm and his family was very poor. They didn't even have a car or a truck. But one day they traded two mules for a car. The only thing was, no one knew how to drive it. Bompie had ridden in cars, though, and he didn't think it could be all that hard to drive one. So Bompie volunteered to go to town to pick up the car and drive it home.

It was raining raining raining. You should hear Sophie tell a story. She really gets into it. You can almost feel the rain on your head when she tells it. You can feel it, you can smell it. It's really something.

Anyway, Bompie goes to pick up the car and it's raining raining raining. He's driving home and he gets to the place where he has to cross the creek. There's no bridge or anything. When they'd walked that way, or ridden the mules, they'd always just waded across it.

So Bompie drives the car into the creek, but the water is rushing, rushing so fast, it's like a big wall of water coming down at him, and Bompie is yelling, 'Hey! *Giddy-up*!' but the car won't *giddy-up*, and that wall of water turns the car over, and Bompie scrambles out and watches the new car float down the stream.

When Bompie finally got home, he got a whipping from his father and an apple pie from his mother.

'Why'd she give him an apple pie?' Brian asked Sophie.

'Because she was grateful that he was alive, that's why,' Sophie said.

'So how do you know this story anyway?' Brian said.

'Hush up, Brian,' Uncle Dock said.

But Sophie said, 'Because Bompie *told* it to me, that's how I know it.'

You could tell Brian wanted to say something else, but he didn't. No one did.

I was sitting there thinking about Bompie getting out of that car and his mother giving him an apple pie.

Today Sophie and Uncle Dock each juggled three pretzel packets for a couple of minutes! They were so excited. I felt pretty good myself. I'm a teacher!

III

The Island

15

Grand Manan

We arrived in Seal Cove on Grand Manan at sunset – was that yesterday? – with the sky awash with streaks of rose and lavender. What a paradise!

I think Uncle Dock knows people everywhere. On our way into Seal Cove, Dock called shore by radio, and the person on shore called a friend of Dock's – Frank is his name – and when we arrived outside the harbour, Frank was there waiting to help guide us in. The harbour is inside a huge breakwall, like a fortress, and *The Wanderer* was the only sailboat scuttling into the harbour where fishing boats were crammed – triple- and quadruple-parked – as if it were a big city parking lot. Frank packed us all in his van and took us to his house a few blocks away, and we met his family and swayed around like dizzy clowns on our wobbly sea legs.

I'm really getting into fish and fishing here. You can't help it; everyone who lives here has something to do with fish. They're fishing for lobsters or pollock or herring, or they're working in the factories that can sardines and herring. Fish, fish, everywhere!

Today we all went lobstering with Frank on his fishing boat, *Frank's Fort*. He'd bought the shell of the boat and built everything else himself. I love it when people do things like that – take something decrepit and create something grand out of it!

Brian doesn't like this sort of thing. He said, 'Sophie, you don't have to go overboard. It's just a boat.'

Just a boat! You could spend months poking around these boats. You'd see buckets of bait, containers full of lobsters, lobster bands to put around the lobsters' claws, hoses, nets and other stuff that gets covered in fish slime and seaweed. Maybe someday I'll be a lobster fisherman; who knows?

Cody said, 'How come you like all this stuff, Sophie?'

'Well, don't you?' I said. 'Don't you like imagining what your life would be like if you were, say, a fisherman? You could smell the sea all day—'

'And smell the fish,' he said. 'You might get sick of fish smell.'

'Or you might think it's the best smell you ever smelled. You might love feeling the air all day and handling the fish and—'

'It's OK, Sophie,' he said. 'You can like this stuff if you want.'

Some of the pots we pulled up were empty, and all that remained of the bait was a perfectly intact snow-white herring skeleton.

'Where'd it go?' I asked.

'Sea fleas,' Frank said. 'They're everywhere, very wee, practically invisible. They love our bait. If you fell overboard and weren't picked up until the next day, those sea fleas would eat you right up, and your skeleton would sink to the bottom!'

Cody lifted me up and hung me over the side. 'Want to try it?' he said.

'Not funny, Cody,' I said. I didn't much like the idea of sea fleas nibbling me down to my bones.

One female lobster was carrying eggs – millions of orange grains (roe, Frank called them) clustered all over the underside of her tail, right up to the head.

'That sweetheart goes back,' Frank said, tossing her overboard. 'To continue the cycle.'

And I had this strange feeling, thinking about how a lobster is saved by being tossed in the ocean, but if I were tossed in the ocean that would be the end of me.

Last night I called home. My mother asked me about two million questions: 'How do you feel? Have you been seasick? Are you warm? Are you safe? Are you scared? Are you lonely?' Finally, my dad took the phone and said, 'What an adventure! What an incredible adventure!'

I'd been feeling fine until I talked with them. My mother made me uneasy, as if she were expecting something awful to go wrong. I kept telling her everything was fine and she shouldn't worry, but when it came time to say goodbye, I could hardly say it. It seemed too final. So I had to say, 'Goodbye *for now*,' and I kept saying '*for now*', until she repeated it, and then I felt better.

My mother also said she'd called Bompie to tell

him we were coming, and 'he sounded all fuzzed up.'

'How do you mean?' I asked.

'He didn't seem to know who I was at first, and he kept calling me Margaret.'

'Margaret? Who is that?'

'Grandma. My mother. His wife. He had me very worried, but then he snapped out of it and he said he was fine, he was just kidding and he was very excited about your visit.'

'Well, then,' I said. 'That's good, right?'

'That's good,' she agreed.

16

Stranded

We are doing a whole lot more stopping than sailing on this trip. It's as if Uncle Dock doesn't really want to get under way. I think there's something funny about all this stopping. Maybe there's something seriously wrong with this boat and only Uncle Dock knows it.

Today I asked Uncle Dock if he knew what had happened to Sophie's parents.

'Nothing,' he said. 'They're back in Kentucky—'

'Not those parents,' I said. 'Her real parents.'

'Ah,' he said.

'Do you know what happened to them?'

'Yep,' he said.

'You gonna tell me?' I asked.

'Nope,' he said.

'Why not?'

'Not a pretty story,' he said.

17

Tradition

Yesterday, Frank's wife told me, 'You're a brave soul to be sailing!' and 'You're a brave soul to be with all of those men!' She asked me if they actually let me do any of the sailing.

'It's a struggle,' I said. 'They don't really want to—'

'I figured that you'd just be doing the cooking and cleaning.'

'No way!' I said. 'That's Cody's job!'

It isn't really Cody's job. We're all supposed to take turns, although Brian usually gets out of it, and Cody does like doing it more than the rest of us. When Frank and his wife visited us on *The Wanderer* and saw Cody doing dishes and mopping the floor, Frank said, 'You'll make a great wife,' and he kept calling Cody 'Mr Mom'.

Cody didn't seem bothered. He made a joke out of it. 'Mr Mom at your service!' he said, bringing them some cheese and crackers, and 'Watch it – Mr Mom needs to mop under your feet!'

I wish I had Cody's natural sense of humour in times like that. I get really antsy when people seem surprised that I can use a power tool or go up a mast or use fibreglass or when they expect me to be the cook. I usually say something snotty and rude back, but I ought to be more like Cody. If you just laugh about it, people drop it.

Yesterday, after we went clamming, Frank turned to me and said, 'You've got a lot of frying to do!'

I said, 'No, I don't! I'm not the only person on board who can cook, you know.'

'Oh,' he said.

I think I hurt his feelings by snapping like that, and I felt bad because he's been so nice to us. I ought to learn to keep my mouth shut sometimes.

I'm going to talk about clamming now. I hope I'm not being too boring with all this, but I want to write it down and remember it all. You could forget things, forget so many details of your life, and then if someone ever wanted to know what you'd thought or what you'd felt, you might not remember, or maybe you'd be sick or gone or something and you couldn't tell them and they'd never know. It would be as if those tiny nibbling sea fleas had eaten up all the substance of your life.

I once asked how Bompie remembered all his stories, and my mother said, 'It's like a picture in his head.'

'But what if the picture got erased?' I said.

'Now, how's that going to happen?' she said.

At low tide, we all went clamming with Frank's seventy-nine-year-old father. We looked for air bubbles in the sand and then started digging, but there was so much seaweed covering the holes, and lots of water, so we couldn't see in the hole once we'd started digging. And the land is mostly rocks and the clams live deep, so the digging wasn't easy.

It's an odd thing, seeing those air bubbles and realizing that something is alive down there, under the sand. I felt peculiar, as if I'd rake up not a clam, but a person.

Brian and Uncle Stew decided that clam digging was no fun after the first twenty minutes. They complained about their jeans getting muddy, and they didn't like to bend over. 'All this digging for one measly clam?' Uncle Stew said.

Frank's father chattered as he worked. 'I was born on this island, just like my parents before me, and I've lived here my whole life, with my twelve brothers and sisters, and all our kids. I clam nearly every day, and I like to putter in the garden too and I hunt deer when I get the chance. Life is good. Real good.'

And I could see how it would be good, how you could stay with your whole big family and everyone would know each other and take care of each other.

I feel as if I can't get enough of life on Grand Manan, and in the midst of learning about Grand Manan, I've learned some things about my uncles too. It's amazing what you pick up while you're standing around clamming or hauling lobster pots.

I discovered that ever since they were kids, Mo, Dock and Stew wanted to sail across the ocean. They talked about it and planned it and dreamed about it.

'Did you ever think you'd really do it?' I asked.

'Nope,' Uncle Mo said.

'What are you talking about?' Uncle Stew said. 'Of course you thought we'd do it. We all thought we'd do it.'

'I didn't,' Mo said.

'But you said – you kept saying – you made us think up all those names for the boat and you kept showing us that atlas, and—'

'It was just a game,' Mo said. 'Wasn't it?'

'A game? A *game*?' Stew spluttered.

'I thought we'd do it,' Uncle Dock said quietly. 'I *knew* we'd do it.'

I asked them if my mother was part of their plans when they were young. 'Did she want to go too?'

'Who?' Uncle Stew said. 'Claire? Is that who you're talking about?'

'Of course it's Claire she's talking about,' Uncle Dock said. 'She wants to know what Claire was like when she was young.'

'Oh,' Uncle Stew said. 'No, Claire didn't want anything to do with us. She thought we were snotty and disgusting.'

'Speak for yourself,' Uncle Dock said. 'Claire and I always got along just fine.'

I also found out that Uncle Mo's name is short for Moses, but that he got beaten up too much when he was a kid ('Think about it,' he said. 'Would you like to be called Moses?') and so he shortened it to Mo, which sounded 'more butch', and he's stuck with it ever since.

And Uncle Dock's real name is Jonah!

'So how'd you go from Jonah to Dock?' I asked him.

'Ever since I was a kid,' he said, 'I loved boats, but one day an old sailor told me that Jonah was not a good name for a sailor to have, because the Jonah in the Bible was bad luck for his companions at sea. You know that story, right? About how Jonah made God mad, so God sent this huge storm—'

'And that's when Jonah got swallowed by the whale,' Brian added.

'Yep, yep, yep. So that old sailor said Jonah wasn't a good name for me, and he started calling me Dock because I hung around the docks all day.'

Brian leaned over and said to me, 'But he's still really a Jonah, so do you think that means bad luck for us?'

'Brian,' I said, 'sometimes you can keep your thoughts in your own head.'

Then I got to worrying that one of us might make God mad and he'd send a storm, and that really seemed to worry me, way out of all proportion, so I started thinking about names instead. I wondered whether you had to be what your name suggested, and how different names suggest different things – like how Brian seems like a Brian, and Cody seems like a Cody, and I wondered if I seemed like a Sophie, and what exactly was a Sophie anyway?

And then I started thinking about Bompie and although I know Bompie is only a nickname, I realized I have no idea what his real name is. I'm going to go ask someone right now.

18

Bompie and the Train

Today when I was grumbling about being stuck on Grand Manan, Sophie said, 'Here's what Bompie told me. It's not where you're going that's important – it's how you get there.'

'Well, we're not getting anywhere, are we?' I said.

'Sure we are!' she said. 'We're on this amazing island. We've been lobstering and we're going clamming. This is part of the trip! We are wanderers!'

I can't figure her out. She can take the smallest thing – like a lobster pot, for instance – and get right up close to it and have a million questions about it and then she wants to draw it and touch it and smell it, and you'd think she'd been locked up in a cage her whole life and had just been let out and was discovering all these amazing things in the world.

To tell you the truth, I didn't think lobsters or lobster pots were all that amazing until Sophie got so excited about them. She kept going on and on about how she might be a lobster fisherman or maybe she'd build boats. You listen to her talk and then you start thinking maybe that *would* be a neat life.

And then you listen to Brian, who says it would be an awful life in the winter and what if you didn't catch anything or what if you built a boat and it sank?

I get mixed up in my head when I listen to the two of them.

I am starting to think something else too. I think Sophie's afraid of the water. It's just a feeling I have.

Brian's still badgering Sophie. When we were clamming, she said that when she'd once been clamming with Bompie, they'd found the clams with their toes, not with a rake. So Brian says, 'That's a lie. You never went clamming with Bompie.'

'Did so,' Sophie said.

'Did not,' Brian said.

'Did so,' Sophie said.

We got to use a phone last night. That was weird. Dad called Mom and barked at her a bit before handing the phone over to me. In her little voice, she said, 'Cody? Cody, honey? You can change your mind if you want. You can come home.'

'Why would I want to do that?' I said. I didn't intend it to sound mean, but I think that's how she took it because she started sniffling. 'Look, Mom,' I said. 'It's fine. We're all fine. Dad sleeps a lot, so he's not on my case so much lately.'

That wasn't exactly the truth, but she doesn't like to hear the truth. I keep wondering why my dad invited me on this trip in the first place. He could have come on his own and he'd have a whole month or more away from me. No aggravation!

*

Here's one good thing about being stranded on land right now: no blah-blah-blah lessons from Brian.

But Sophie did tell us another Bompie story when we were out clamming. It went like this:

When Bompie was about my age, he lived near the Ohio River, at a place where the river was very deep and a mile wide. Running across the river was a train track, and it was only for trains and there were warnings all over the place about how people shouldn't step one foot on it because there was no way to get off if a train was coming.

One day Bompie wanted to get across that river. He wanted to get over to the other side real bad. It was windy and rainy and he didn't want to walk two miles down to the pedestrian bridge. So he started across the train tracks.

You should hear Sophie tell this story. You feel as if you're there with Bompie, looking down at that river, with the wind blowing in your face and the rain slithering down the back of your neck and inside your shirt.

So Bompie is walk walk walking across this bridge and he gets to the middle, and guess what he hears? Well, I guessed what he was going to hear the minute Sophie said that he was going to walk on that train track. He heard the train. Sophie described that train rumbling off in the distance, and you could feel the vibrations on the track and see Bompie looking back, knowing that train was going to come looming around the bend any minute.

He was in the middle of the bridge. He started to run towards the far side, telling himself '*Giddy-up, giddy-up!*' but the rocks on the side of the tracks were slippery and he was having a hard time keeping his balance and he couldn't *giddy-up*. And the rumbling got louder and louder and he could feel those vibrations and then there it was, the big black engine bursting around that bend and aiming for that trestle bridge.

Bompie knew he wasn't going to make it to the other side in time. He crawled up on the ledge and squeezed through the steel supports and dangled over the side of the bridge. The water was a long long long way down, swirling and brown and muddy.

And the train, loud and rumbling, came surging towards him, and he let go and down down down he fell into the swirling water.

Sophie stopped then and looked at each of us.

'Well?' we all asked. 'Well? What happened next?'

'Oh, it was a terrible struggle,' Sophie said. 'Bompie was upside down in that deep muddy swirling river. He figured his time was up.'

'Well?' we asked. 'And *then* what?'

So she told how Bompie finally spluttered to the surface, and he was so happy to see the sky that he lay there floating on his back, crying and laughing all at the same time, and the current was sweeping him down the river, and he floated there and watched the train go by and finally he turned over and swam like a madman, he swam and swam and swam, and he made it to shore.

And when he got home, his father gave him a whipping for getting his clothes wet and muddy, and his mother gave him some apple pie.

When she finished telling this story, Brian said, 'I thought you said Bompie grew up in England.'

'I didn't say that,' Sophie said. 'I said he was *born* in

England. He left there when he was very young. Five, I think.'

'Huh!' Brian said.

'Don't you know anything about your own grandfather?' Sophie said.

19

Wood Island

I'm all mixed up about the days.

And mercy! Bompie's name is Ulysses! Although everyone in the family calls him Bompie, apparently some of his friends call him by his real name. It's hard for me to imagine that. *Ulysses*?

We're still on Grand Manan, and sometimes I am longing, longing to get under way again, and I am longing to see Bompie (Ulysses!), but at other times, I get hypnotized by this island and the life here and forget that time is passing or that I've ever lived anywhere else or have anywhere else to go.

Yesterday, Cody and I met a tall, lanky woman and her German shepherd. She showed us her cabin, tucked in a scrub of trees. It was very small, one room, with no water or electricity.

'Built it myself,' she said.

'You mean everything?' I asked. 'You mean you dug the foundation and you hammered it all together – how'd you do that? And the roof? And the windows?'

'Steady on,' she said. 'Too many questions.'

I wanted to be that woman. I could see myself

living out there in that cabin with my dog. In the daytime, I'd go lobstering and clamming.

'You don't get lonely out here?' I asked.

'Lonely? Ha! Lonely? Not by a long shot. I've got my dog, and when I want to see people I just walk down to the harbour. When I want *real* quiet, I go on over to Wood Island.'

Wood Island, she told us, is about a twenty-minute dinghy trip from Seal Cove. 'The few houses there were abandoned,' she said, 'and now there's only a couple of hermits over there, and ghosts—'

'Ghosts?' Cody said. 'You mean like real ghosts?' He seemed very intrigued by this.

'Hm,' she said. 'What exactly is a real ghost?'

One of the ghosts, she said, is an old man who roams around in a black raincoat and a black hat; and the other is a woman and her baby who float around singing spooky songs.

'Why are they there?' I asked.

'What do you mean?' the woman said.

'I mean why are those ghosts in that place and not, say, here?'

'Honey, you sure have a lot of questions!' she said. But you could tell she was thinking because she was nodding her head and tilting it this way and that. Finally she said, 'Those ghosts are coming back to a place they once lived. Maybe they forgot something.'

I liked this idea, that the ghosts might come back to check on something they'd left behind.

Today, Cody and I took off in the dinghy in search

of the ghosts and hermits. The fog was thick as smoke, so by the time we were four hundred feet out of the breakwall, we were out of sight of land altogether. We took with us a few items for emergency survival: a compass, a flashlight, three cans of pop and half a bag of candy. We drank the pop on the way over and ate the candy within five minutes of landing on Wood Island.

There are no roads on Wood Island, only paths that lead from deserted house to deserted house. We found a church, though, which was cleanly swept and dusted, with fresh wild flowers and candles at the altar.

'Maybe the ghosts come here and tidy it up,' Cody said.

I knelt down and said a little prayer for Bompie and for my parents and for my boat family and our journey across the ocean.

Cody said, 'What'd you pray for?' and when I told him, he knelt down and closed his eyes, and I think he said a little prayer too.

In one deserted house Cody discovered a bead necklace that was gnarled and broken.

'For you,' Cody said, gallantly presenting me with the tangled string and loose beads. 'Maybe you can restring it?'

And when he put the beads in my hand, they were warm, and I felt as if there were other people in the house with us, maybe they were ghosts, and I wondered what had happened to them, and was this all that was left of their lives?

On we went, hoping to find a ghost or a hermit,

but the only people we saw were two men building a house across the path from the church. One of them called out to us. 'I guess your clothes won't be drying too well in this weather, will they?'

'Huh?' Cody said. 'What do you mean?'

'On your boat,' he said, 'back in the harbour – all your clothes strung up on the lifelines. Too much fog for clothes to be drying, eh?'

'How did you know that was our boat and our clothes?' Cody asked.

They laughed. 'Not too many strangers around these parts, nope.'

Cody thought they were being nosy, but I liked it that they'd noticed we were there. We weren't invisible.

We headed for the centre of the island, deep in moss and rotted leaves and trees. It was like walking through snow. Our feet sank in the mushy carpeting, and every once in a while we broke through to muddy swampiness underneath.

It was all so quiet and peaceful. There was open sky, with no power lines or phone lines or fluorescent street lights. We heard only birds, with no sounds of cars or lawnmowers blaring. I started picturing myself living on the island. I could fix up one of those cabins and I'd live there with my dog, and maybe all the people who used to live there would come back, one by one, and fill up their houses and their lives all over again.

Shortly before sunset, we left Wood Island. The fog

was much thicker, and we could barely scc twenty feet in front of the bow of the dinghy. I couldn't imagine how we'd ever find our way back, and I had a sudden panicky feeling, as if the fog was choking me.

'Breathe deeply!' Cody said. 'Don't worry – I've got the compass! Commander Compass at your service!' He switched places with me. 'You row, I'll guide,' he said. 'Head a little left – no, not that way, your right, my left – OK now straight on, *giddy-up*, steady, you're veering, OK a little more right – no, your left, my right—'

All I saw was fog, fog, fog. Fog shrinks the ocean. You feel as if you are in a tiny sphere of mist and water.

'Steady on, we're OK, we're right on course,' Cody said. 'Onward!'

I rowed harder and harder and faster and faster to keep us from disappearing. On we went, on and on through the fog, until at last Cody shouted, 'Ahoy! Fortress!'

And there we were, back at the mouth of the breakwall. Safe. Cody knows some things, after all.

When we reached the dock, Uncle Mo and Brian and Uncle Stew were with a fisherman on his boat, ready to go out to find us.

'Where the heck have you knuckleheads been?' Uncle Mo demanded.

'On Wood Island, exactly where we said we'd be,' Cody said.

'This man says he was out there and he didn't see hide nor hair of you. Isn't that right?'

The man nodded. 'Yup, that's right. I been out there all day and you weren't there.'

'We were,' Cody said. 'We were exploring.'

Apparently the fisherman had told Uncle Mo about the four-knot current that runs between Grand Manan and Wood Island, and he'd pulled out a chart and showed Uncle Mo how we'd be drifting far below Grand Manan in the Bay of Fundy, freezing, starving and about to be run over by a freighter.

'Well, we weren't,' Cody said. 'We weren't lost and we weren't drifting or freezing or starving or run over by a freighter.'

'But you could've been,' Uncle Mo said.

'But we weren't,' Cody said.

Now I've been sitting here thinking. I wonder how easily it could have all gone wrong, and what if we had drifted out into the Bay of Fundy, and what if, what if, what if . . .?

And I wonder why I didn't worry about these things beforehand. Maybe it was because I didn't know about the four-knot current and I didn't know about the bad things that could happen. I wondered if it was better to know about the bad things in advance and worry about them, or whether it was better not to know, so that you could enjoy yourself.

My brain is tossing these thoughts back and forth and making me antsy. I'm not going to think about them any more.

20

The Little Kid

Sophie loves to explore, so we've been poking around and even got rid of Brian long enough to row over to Wood Island. When we were in an abandoned house, she wanted to pick up every little thing she saw, as if every little piece of rubbish was a treasure or a clue. 'Who do you think owned this?' she said, and 'Why do you think they left?'

She poked at the walls and said, 'I could live here. If I had to.'

Later, when we were exploring the middle of the island, I felt as if ghosts were hovering around us. The woman ghost and the baby ghost were following us through the woods, and I kept asking Sophie if she saw them, but she didn't.

She said, 'I don't believe in ghosts. I think they're all in your mind.'

On we went along the mossy path. I got brave. 'Sophie,' I said, 'can I ask you something about your parents?'

'Sure,' she said.

'What really happened to them?'

She didn't stop, didn't hesitate, didn't even skip a beat. It was as if she and Uncle Dock had rehearsed the same answer. She said, 'Nothing happened to them. They're back in Kentucky—'

'Not them,' I said. 'Your other—'

'My parents are back in Kentucky,' she said. 'You want to race to that rock up there?' and she took off running.

What is up with her?

When we got to the other side of the rock, she started talking about this little kid she knows. She said this little kid had lived a lot of places.

'How many?' I said.

'A lot, a lot, a lot. Some not-so-nice places.'

'Where were the little kid's parents?'

'Somewhere else. So the little kid had to live with other people. They didn't really want the little kid. The little kid was always in the way. You want to race all the way over there? To that scrabbly tree?'

When we got back my father was having a humongous fit about how irresponsible we'd been and how we could have been dragged out into the ocean and all that jazz. He doesn't give me credit for beans. I was getting really ticked, but then Sophie tugged at my arm and whispered, 'At least he was worried about you.'

'He sure has a funny way of showing it,' I said. 'All that yelling and all.'

And Brian asked me about a million questions. He wanted to know where we went and how we got there and what we saw and why we didn't tell him we were going and were we scared coming back and what if we'd gotten lost and about a thousand other questions like that.

I almost felt bad that we hadn't invited him, but then he said that he was going to make up lists of what each person was doing each day so that someone would know each person's whereabouts.

'And why would we want to know that?' I asked him.

'Because!' he said. 'Because we ought to know where everybody is, don't you think? In case someone got lost or hurt or something. Then if they didn't come back, somebody would know they were missing and somebody would know where they were supposed to be and somebody—'

'You're such a worrier,' I said.

'But he's got a point,' Sophie said. She turned to Brian. 'It's a good idea, Brian.'

Brian turned about seventeen shades of red and shambled off looking mighty pleased with himself.

'Geez, Sophie,' I said. 'You think that nerd-brain had a good idea?'

'If he wants to know where everybody is, then he must care what happens to everybody. We must matter to him.' And then she turned around and went over to the railing and stared out at the water, and I felt about as sad as I've ever felt in my whole life.

21

The Baptism

The sea, the sea, the sea. It rolls and rolls and calls to me. *Come in*, it says, *come in*.

Uncle Dock is forecasting tomorrow or the next day as the Day of Departure. 'Just a few more things to fix,' he says. I feel torn, as if something is pushing and pulling. I could stay forever on Grand Manan, but the sea is calling me.

This morning, Cody, Brian and I went to a boat-building place, where the man who owns it let us nose around. He works mostly in fibreglass, hand-laying everything, even the gel coat. He even makes his own dinghies, and his work is so fine. I thought I knew something about fibreglass from building Buddy the Bilge Box, but I hardly know potatoes.

'Look at this,' Brian felt obliged to mention. 'Not a bubble in sight.'

'Well, he's been doing it longer than I have,' I said.

The man showed me some tricks, like how to use rollers to apply the resin and gel coat, and how to use plastic wrap on small areas so the layers underneath stay smooth.

'That's what you should've done with Buddy the Bilge Box,' Brian said.

'I didn't know about that then, did I?' I said. Brian was starting to bug me.

'You don't like me, do you?' Brian asked.

That made me feel awful. 'I never said that.'

'It's OK if you don't. No one does.' He stood there like a limp puppet, all clumsy arms and legs.

Cody was taking this all in, listening but not saying anything.

'I have no idea why nobody likes me,' Brian said.

I was hoping he wasn't going to ask me to give him some reasons, when Cody piped up.

'Well,' Cody said, 'it might have something to do with all those lists you make and how you're always telling everybody what to do and how you always act like you have the answers to every single little atom of a thing and—'

Brian folded his arms tightly across his chest. 'I wasn't talking to you,' he said. 'I don't care what you think,' and he turned and left the building, striding along in his jerky, stumbling way.

'Well, he asked for it,' Cody said.

Uncle Dock made us all go to the baptism for Frank's grandson later in the day. Brian stayed as far away from me and Cody as he could get. I didn't want to go at all; my heart was not in it, but I'd never been to a baptism before, and by the time it was over, my eyes were bugging out of my head.

People in robes, sort of like graduation robes, walked into the water, waist deep, with a pastor.

The pastor dunked them, *sploosh*, backwards, full body, into the cold, cold water. It looked as if the pastor was holding them down, and what if they couldn't breathe, what if he held them down too long?

All the while the people were being dunked, the bystanders were singing *Amazing Grace*, and that song made me freeze up completely. Where had I heard that song before? At a funeral? My throat was all clogged, as if there was something stuck in it, like a big sock. Everything got blurry and woozy, and Uncle Dock said, 'Sophie? Sophie? You'd better sit. Put your head down—'

On the way over to Frank's house for the baptism feast, Brian broke his silence to inform us that the reason for the dunking was that the water would cleanse them of all their sins and they could start fresh, as whole, new, clean people. I kept thinking and thinking about that, and what I saw in my head was this very dirty person being dipped and then *whoosh* out he came all white and clean, like an angel. I saw this over and over and I started getting dizzy and woozy again.

'Here,' Uncle Dock said. 'Eat some of this. Maybe you haven't eaten enough today,' and he offered me some seafood chowder and fried scallops and lobster salad sandwiches and potato salad and two kinds of cheesecake and carrot cake and banana bread. I ate what I could but then I threw it all up.

'Maybe you've got the flu,' Uncle Dock said, and he took me back to the boat.

I slept a bit and then woke up when Brian and Cody came in.

Brian said, 'I hope that wasn't our last supper.'

'Shut *up*!' Cody shouted. 'You're such a wet blanket. Why do you always expect the worst? What are you trying to do, jinx our voyage?'

'I'd feel a whole lot better if the crew on this boat actually knew what they were doing,' Brian sneered.

'Well, you're part of the crew, you knuckleheaded doofus—'

'*I'm* not a knuckleheaded doofus – you are!'

Our boat family is getting touchy and nervous. We're all ready to be under way, but we're also starting to think of the problems we might encounter. Thinking too much is not good. We should just *go*!

22

Bompie and the Pastor

I am losing my brains. We're still here, still on Grand Manan, and now we have to fix a bunch more things on *The Wanderer*. Is this boat seaworthy or not?

Yesterday, I came across Uncle Dock and his friend Frank, huddled by the shore, talking. When they saw me, Uncle Dock said to Frank, 'Shh. Enough of that.' He waved his hand in the air, as if he were swishing flies. 'What's up, Cody?' Whatever they'd been talking about, they didn't want me to hear.

Here's something else weird: when I came back to the boat tonight and went below deck, my father was lying on his bunk crying. Crying! The tears were streaming down his face.

'Something wrong?' I asked him.

He didn't even wipe his face. He just said, 'No. Nothing wrong. Everything's just usual.' That's all he said.

I have never, ever, ever, ever in my whole entire life, seen my father cry. Once when I was about eight and I came home crying because I'd fallen off my bike, he said, 'Stop it! You don't have to cry about it!' And when I didn't stop crying, he went berserk. 'Stop it! Stop it! Stop it!' He whipped off his belt and waved it at me. 'You want something to cry about? I'll give you something to—'

My mother came tiptoeing in the back door and when she saw that belt, she tried to grab it, but my father is a strong man and he snapped it back and hit her with it, right on her bare arm. Then he threw the belt on the floor and stormed outside.

I don't cry in front of him any more.

Sophie told her Bompie-gets-baptized story. It went like this:

Bompie was a teenager and he'd never been baptized and his mother thought he really really really needed to be baptized and so she arranged with the local pastor to do the baptism in the Ohio River.

Bompie and the pastor did not get along very well because Bompie had been dating the pastor's daughter and brought her home late too many times. Bompie was not exactly thrilled at the idea that this pastor was going to dunk him in the river.

Comes the day and Bompie goes down to the river with his family, and there's the pastor smiling a big phony smile at Bompie, and comes the time for Bompie to get dunked, and the pastor slams Bompie down into the muddy swirling water and holds him there. And holds him there. And holds him there some more. And Bompie is running out of breath so he starts kicking the pastor and then he bites the pastor's hand, which is covering Bompie's mouth.

And the pastor let out a shout and Bompie got to the surface.

'Well?' Brian said. 'What did Bompie's father do?'

Sophie said, 'Why, he gave Bompie a whipping for biting the pastor.'

'And his mother?' I said. 'Did she give Bompie some apple pie?'

'Why, I believe she did,' Sophie said.

My father cried again today.

'Anything wrong?' I asked him.

'No,' he said. 'Nothing's wrong. Everything's usual.'

I just remembered something else about Sophie telling the Bompie baptism story yesterday. When she was finished, Brian said, 'So, Dad, you ever heard that story before?'

'No,' Uncle Stew said, 'can't say that I have.'

Brian looked smug, as if he'd just swallowed a watermelon. Uncle Dock said, 'I haven't either—'

'So!' Brian said.

Uncle Dock interrupted. 'But that one about the train and the river – that one rang a bell, yep. I believe I might've heard that one before.'

I thought Brian was going to choke on his phantom watermelon.

Uncle Stew said, 'Well, I haven't heard it. Haven't heard any of them—'

'Maybe you forgot,' Uncle Dock said.

'I don't forget anything!'

'Maybe Bompie never told you,' Uncle Dock said.

'Why would he tell you and not me?' Uncle Stew was getting very red in the face. 'Mo?' he said. 'You heard this story before?'

'Nope,' my dad said.

'See?' Uncle Stew said.

'But then,' my dad said, 'that one about the car in the river – that one sounded familiar.'

'Nobody ever tells me anything!' Uncle Stew said.

The whole time this was going on, Sophie just sat there juggling pretzel packets.

IV

Under Way

23

Whoosh!

The sea, the sea, the sea!

Yesterday afternoon, Cody came running down the dock saying, 'Uncle Dock's says it's zero hour. Get your stuff. We're going.'

'You mean *now*?' I said. 'Like right this minute?'

'Yep!' He was grinning his wide, wide grin. 'This is it, Sophie!'

I ran around getting my stuff and didn't have a whole lot of time to think about what was happening or how I felt about it, but here we are, we are on our way! *Whoosh*, we are off!

The first couple of hours were frenzied, with everyone double-checking his own stuff and arguing over space, and Uncle Stew and Brian handing out assignments and schedules and trying their best to make me feel like a slug, but I was having none of it, and I kept my cool and didn't even get too snotty with them.

As we were leaving the Bay of Fundy, we heard a *plop* and another *plop* and *plop plop plop!* Surrounding us were dozens of seals, sticking their sweet faces out of the water to have a look around.

'Hey, there, darlin'—' Cody said, as they twitched their whiskers at us. Even Brian seemed taken with them; for once he didn't have a bossy comment to make. He sat on deck with his hands cupped under his chin, watching the seals.

Uncle Mo sat on the aft deck, sketching. I like his drawings. He showed me how the seals that are farther away should appear smaller in the drawing than the ones closer up. I tried to draw them too, but my drawing wasn't as good as Uncle Mo's.

'Are you an artist?' I asked him.

'Me?' he said. 'No.'

'But you look like an artist to me,' I said. 'You draw really good stuff.'

'Naw,' he said. 'This isn't so hot. I'm pretty rusty.'

I asked him what his job was, what he did for a living. He frowned. 'I'm a number-cruncher. I sit at a computer all day and mess around with numbers.'

'But did you want to be an artist?' I asked. 'Before you were a number-cruncher?'

'Sure,' he said.

'So why didn't you?'

'Why didn't I what?' Mo said. He was putting whiskers on the seals in his drawing.

'Be an artist. Why didn't you become an artist instead of a number-cruncher?'

He used his finger to smudge the water line in his drawing, making it look soft and fuzzy and more like water. I thought maybe he hadn't heard me, but finally he said, 'I dunno. Why does anybody become anything?'

'Isn't it because they want to?' I asked. 'Don't you become what you want to become?'

He looked at me. His mouth was partly open and

it seemed like there were words in there but they couldn't come out. He closed his mouth and tried again. 'Not usually, Sophie. That's not the way it works usually.'

'But why not? Why wouldn't a person do what he was good at and what he wanted to do?'

Now Uncle Mo was drawing ripples around the seals. 'Because sometimes, Sophie, a person just needs a job. And sometimes the job he can get is not the one he most wants.'

'Well, I hope I don't do that,' I said. 'I hope I don't get a job I don't want. It seems like such a waste.'

'Ah,' Uncle Mo said, putting away his drawing. 'Youth.'

There was no moon that first night, and it was eerie, so dark, the sky and the sea folding a huge black blanket around us. I saw a sparkle and a flash in the water, and then more sparkles and flashes, little streams of light trailing beside the boat, as if the lights were little beacons from someone lost down below.

'Phosphorescent plankton!' Uncle Dock said. 'Beauteous!'

All along the sides of the boat, little spots flashed all night, like underwater fireflies. It seemed magical and mysterious, as if they were sending me a message in code. I wanted so badly to decode their message, but I couldn't, and I got yelled at because I was so busy watching the flashing fish-lights that I wasn't paying attention to the sails.

Later that night, as we were pushing out into the open ocean, we heard a loud rushing of water, a spewing and bellowing. Whales! It was too dark to see them, but one blew so close to us that I nearly shinnied up the mast. It sounded huge, gargantuan!

Sometimes when I think about what is happening, I get the cold shivers. We're crossing the ocean! And now we won't be able to get off the boat and walk around. There will be no new people to meet, no new foods to try, no time alone, no land, no fresh water, no trees, no exercise except boat exercise. And how will we all get along, cooped up like this, with no chance to get away from each other?

I'm worried about being cooped up with Uncle Mo because he is often so loud, and he and Cody seem always on the verge of knocking each other's block off. And then there's Uncle Stew and Brian, always bossing everyone about and fussing over things and making me feel very, very small. Uncle Dock is the calmest, and the one I feel most comfortable around, but sometimes he seems disorganized and so worried about what might happen that I wonder if he's really going to let us carry on, or if he will make us turn back when he finds the first leak or broken bit.

But all of those worries are countered by this huge, surging, pushing feeling, as if the sea is calling and the wind is pushing and *whoosh* off we are going, *whoosh!* And you feel as if this is where you should be and you wonder where you are going and you can't even think because *whoosh*, you are off, *whoosh!*

Boom! Thunder now! The weather report calls for hail and strong winds – whoa! That'll liven things up, for sure.

24

Oranges and Pizza

Un-be-liev-able! We are actually on our way!

It's raining, but who cares? We have wind and are sailing along! I was standing up on deck letting the wind splosh my face and I was looking up at the sails and I thought it was the prettiest sight I'd ever seen. You feel so *free*!

Caught my dad practising juggling with oranges today! When he saw me watching, he dropped the oranges, and said, 'It's stupid, juggling.'

I've been sitting here thinking about the night before we left Grand Manan, when my father and I called Mom to say goodbye (again). She sounded awfully cheery. Maybe she's getting used to being on her own, without anyone hassling her.

Dad's end of the conversation was weird, not his usual barking self. He kept saying 'I know,' and 'I will,' and 'It's OK,' and little two-word sentences like that. At the end, he got kind of choked up (this is my father??) and told her he loved her.

Man!

When he hung up the phone, he said, 'Want a pizza?'

25

Fired

The sea!

We're doing two-person watches right now, and I'm on with Uncle Dock again, which is good, except that he doesn't like to steer if it's raining, and it has been raining since we left. He wants to use the autohelm, but I'd rather steer the whole time than use that thing. I feel as if we're more in control of where we're going if someone is actually steering.

The wind has been good and steady, and so far we're making good time. It would be nice if it would stop raining, but when I'm feeling cold and miserable, I remember something Bompie once said: 'Suffering builds character.' He said that if you are always lolling around and being pampered and life is too easy, then you turn into a spineless wimp, but if you encounter suffering, you learn to face challenges and you get stronger. It sounds like something a grandparent might say, doesn't it?

This morning, when I was in the forecabin getting dressed, I heard Uncle Dock and Uncle Stew talking in the galley. Uncle Stew didn't sound like his normal bossy self. His voice was all scratchy and his words were stumbling out.

'I don't know why – I had no idea – it was out of the blue – I was good at that job—'

'You'll find something else,' Uncle Dock said.

'What if I don't?' Uncle Stew said. 'I shouldn't have come. I should be out there looking for a job—'

'This is the best thing for you,' Uncle Dock said. 'Trust me.'

I was shocked. Uncle Stew got fired? That's what it sounded like, anyway. When I came out of the cabin, Uncle Stew turned away from me, hiding his face.

'Hey there, Sophie,' Uncle Dock said. 'Brian's been calling for you—'

'Why? The toilet need cleaning?' I said. It was just a joke but I was sorry I said it, because Uncle Stew probably didn't need to hear me talking like that about Brian when he was sitting there feeling so miserable about losing his job.

26

Code

Here's a weird thing. My dad gave his first lesson in radio code. I thought it was going to be mega-boring and that he would be a grouchy teacher, but you can tell he really likes this stuff and it was actually interesting. It's like secret code. And it's something that Mr Know-it-all Brian and his know-it-all father don't know yet, so we're all learning it at the same time. I am going to learn it first and I am going to learn it better. So there, Mr Know-it-all!

It's so cool, this radio code thing. Each letter of the alphabet has a word that goes with it, like this:

A is Alpha
B is Bravo
C is Charlie
D is Delta
E is Echo

And on like that. So if you say the word *dad*, for instance, and you want to make sure the person on the other end hears you correctly, you say, 'Dad: Delta-Alpha-Delta.' Is that cool or what?

27

Insurance

The sea, the sea, the sea. It rolls and rolls and calls to me! All day long it changes colour, from blue to black to grey and all the shades in between, and I love the sea, I love the sea!

The Wanderer has been keeping good speed so far, and we're now on a good beam reach straight ahead – across we go! Most of our watch time is taken up with trimming sails and keeping a steady course, and our off-watch time is filled with cleaning and cooking and keeping things in order (this makes Brian and Uncle Stew happy).

Last night we spoke with another vessel on the radio; it was a lone sailor having electrical trouble and he needed to know where he was. He didn't need other assistance, but all night I kept thinking about him out there on his own. Was he glad to be on his own, or was he afraid?

When I came off watch, Uncle Stew was talking to the sailor on the radio again.

'Didn't you sleep?' I asked Uncle Stew.

'Naw – just trying to figure out how this thing works, that's all.'

He didn't fool me. He was worried about the sailor too.

I said, 'If you think this is too nosy, you don't have to answer, but I was wondering. What do you do – what's your job – when you're working?'

He didn't look up at me. 'When I'm working, I sell insurance.'

'You mean like life insurance and car insurance and stuff like that?'

'Yes,' he said. 'You can never have too much insurance.'

'I don't get how that life insurance works,' I said. 'You pay money to insure what – that you stay alive? How is paying money going to help you stay alive? And if you don't stay alive – well, what good is the insurance?'

Uncle Stew rubbed his forehead. I was probably giving him a headache. 'It's kind of complicated,' he said. 'The insurance helps the people who are left behind.'

'So do you like doing that?' I asked.

'Doing what?'

'Selling insurance.'

'Not really. Anyway, I got fired.'

'Well, maybe that's a good thing,' I said. 'Now you can do what you really want.'

'Huh,' he said.

'What would that be?' I asked. 'What do you really really want to do?'

'You know what, Sophie?' Uncle Stew said. 'I have no idea. No idea whatsoever. Isn't that pitiful?'

'Yep,' I said. Well, it was true. It sounded really pitiful to me.

*

The waves have been slowly getting bigger, and the forecabin bounces around like a roller coaster. When I was asleep in there, I dreamed I was not yet born and my mother was running a marathon. All this rocking motion makes me so sleepy, and it is tempting to spend all my off-watch time snuggled up in my narrow bunk, but I'd get in trouble if I did. Brian or Uncle Stew would be jabbing me and telling me about my assignments.

Cody has been learning about ham radio, and Uncle Dock surprised me by saying that my father was trying to get a single sideband antenna hooked up, and if he did, we could be in touch with him via the ham radio. In a way, I loved that idea, thinking that I'd still be in touch, but I was also disappointed because it seemed as if it would be cheating, as if I'd be getting extra help or something.

I've been thinking about Bompie, carrying on conversations with him in my head. 'Here we come, Bompie! Sailing over the mighty seas to the rolling green hills of England. Here we come!'

28

Charlie-Oscar-Delta-Yankee

Whoo! We are moving along! No detours! Spooky fog out there, though, makes everything look like a horror movie. You expect some big monster to come looming up out of the deep and swallow you up.

Learned more radio code. Here's the whole alphabet:

A Alpha
B Bravo
C Charlie
D Delta
E Echo
F Foxtrot
G Golf
H Hotel
I India
J Juliet
K Kilo
L Lima
M Mike
N November
O Oscar
P Papa
Q Quebec
R Romeo

S Sierra
T Tango
U Uniform
V Victor
W Whiskey
X X-ray
Y Yankee
Z Zulu

So here's my name in radio code: Cody: Charlie-Oscar-Delta-Yankee. Is that cool or what?

And my dad's name, Mo, becomes: Mike-Oscar.

And Sophie is Sierra-Oscar-Papa-Hotel-India-Echo.

We've been calling each other Charlie-Oscar and Mike-Oscar and Sierra-Oscar for practice.

'You seen Mike-Oscar?'

'I think he's up on deck with Sierra-Oscar.'

Like that.

Brian's name becomes: Bravo-Romeo-India-Alpha-November. So we've been calling him Bravo-Romeo. 'Oh Romeo! Bravo-Romeo!' He actually laughed. Brian *laughed.*

Learned a cool knot from Sierra-Oscar-Papa-Hotel-India-Echo (Sophie). It's called a clove hitch.

I just practised on my shoelaces. Tied them to a pole down below deck. Got yelled at. 'What the heck are you doing tying your shoes to a pole while you've still got your shoes on your feet?' Uncle Stew shouted. 'What if you had to get up in a hurry?'

'I'd kick my shoes off,' I said.

29

Blips

Here we are, well out in the big blue, rolling, rolling, sailing on to England. Out here, I feel as if the ocean is alive, as if it is living and breathing and moody, oh so moody! Sometimes it is calm and smooth, as if it were asleep; and sometimes it is playful, splashing and rolling; and sometimes it is angry and knocks us about. It's as if the ocean has many sides, like me.

We spent yesterday in major work mode because two grommets on the mainsail tore out. Uncle Stew and Brian fluttered around trying to find someone to blame. Apparently whoever let out the sail (Uncle Stew says it was Cody; Cody says it was Brian) forgot to also let out the outhaul line, so the tension was too great along one side of the sail and *pop* went the grommets.

Grommets. Slides. Outhaul. I already knew what these words meant, but Cody cannot get them in his head – or if he can, he refuses to use the right words. He calls the grommets *hole thingys* and the slides *metal thingys* and the outhaul *that line thingy.* He and Uncle Stew had a major fight yesterday when

Cody was telling him about the *hole thingys* tearing and coming away from the *metal-slide thingys*.

'What the heck are you talking about?' Uncle Stew yelled at Cody. 'You sound like an idjit. You don't belong on this boat if you can't learn the proper names for things.'

'I know what I'm doing, even if I don't call things by their la-dee-dah names,' Cody said.

'There's a reason why everything has a name,' Uncle Stew insisted. He was poking Cody's shoulder with his finger. 'What are you going to say in an emergency? "*Help! The hole thingy is loose!*"?'

'Quit poking me,' Cody said.

Their arguing roused Uncle Mo from his bunk down below. 'You calling my son an idjit?' Uncle Mo demanded.

Uncle Stew reeled around and faced Uncle Mo. 'I said he *sounds* like an idjit half the time—'

'So you're calling him an idjit? And you think that wimpy son of yours is smarter than my son? Is that what you're saying?' Then Uncle Mo started jabbing *his* finger at Uncle Stew.

Uncle Stew pushed Uncle Mo. 'Brian has more brains in his little toe than Cody has in his whole idjit body!'

I think they were just about to toss a few blows when Uncle Dock intervened.

'Knock it off,' Uncle Dock said. 'There isn't room on this boat for grown men to be acting like spoiled kids.'

'You calling me a spoiled kid?' Uncle Mo shouted.

'Yep,' Uncle Dock said.

Uncle Mo sucked in a load of air and sputtered it out and turned around to Cody and said, 'Why do you always have to start something?'

'Me?' Cody said.

'Yes, you,' Uncle Mo said. 'Now get down below and start making lunch!'

Cody just shook his head and went down below, and Uncle Mo followed him. I heard them yelling at each other for a while, and then it was quiet, and pretty soon they brought lunch up for the rest of us, and everyone sat around not looking at each other, just eating lunch and trying to forget the fight.

This morning we saw the sun for the first time since we left Grand Manan, and it sure was a welcome sight. Sun, sun, sun! Beautiful, brilliant sun! Everyone wanted to be on deck, worshipping it. It wrapped us all in the most brilliant light and warmed our faces and our bones; it dried our clothes; it flickered along the waves.

The repair work we had to do was easier with the sun beaming down on us. We took down the mainsail, dried off the ripped grommet holes and put strips of sticky-back sail tape around the sides of the sail to cover the holes. The sail tape wasn't sticky enough, though, so I stitched along the sides to keep them secure.

Brian couldn't resist saying, 'It's a good thing we have a girl aboard so she can sew things.'

Grrrr. Sewing sails is heavy work! The material is stiff and thick, and you have to use special needles and a palm thimble to push the needle through.

After I stitched the sails, Cody and I punched new holes through the sailcloth and put in new brass grommets. Cody lashed some thin line through the new grommet holes to the slides, and we were done.

In full hearing of Uncle Stew, Cody said, 'Look, Sierra-Oscar. We done fixed up the hole thingys and now they'll work on the metal thingys easy peasy.' He smiled at Uncle Stew, and before Uncle Stew could erupt, Cody said, 'And, Sierra-Oscar, if you want to use fancy words, you can call these hole thingys *grommets* and you can call these metal thingys *slides*.'

Before we raised the sail again, Cody noticed that the outhaul line ('the line thingy, but if you want to use its fancy word you should call it an *outhaul line*,' he said) up by the boom was chafing, so I got my bosun's chair and harness and hooked myself up to the halyard, and Cody hauled me up. Usually I try to haul myself up, but when the waves are big, you just want to concentrate on not smashing into the mast.

As soon as I was a couple of inches off the deck, I was flying out over the waves, swinging in my chair, while the boat tossed and turned like a runaway seesaw. You swing out over the rolling waves, and the boat rolls and the waves roll and you roll, and you are up in the air in the wind, flying along!

I taped up the line as slowly as I could so that I'd have as much time up there as possible.

'What's the matter, Sophie?' Uncle Stew called. 'Having trouble? Can't do it?'

'I'm doing just fine, Sierra-Tango-Echo-Whiskey,' I said. I was just about to add 'you idjit' to that, but then I looked down on him and he looked so small below, small and rumpled and a little pitiful, so I swallowed the 'idjit' part.

Our fish count is zero. I don't know what we're doing wrong. I'm relieved, though. I hated killing those fish.

But we've seen birds (where do they come from?) and they *love* the lures. Today a gull tried to make a grab for the lure but instead got tangled in the line. Cody made a dramatic rescue, pulling the bird on deck and untangling the line from around its wing and then gently placing it back in the water.

'Bye-bye, birdie,' Cody called as it floated away.

We also saw dolphins last night and again this morning – three of them leaping and diving, having a grand time.

'Hello-oooo, darlings!' Cody called.

I love to see the dolphins. I feel as if they are messengers. For me.

This morning's sun didn't last long, and now there is rain, rain, more rain. We've also had serious fog at night, but good wind.

Last night in the fog, when Brian and I were scanning the radar, we spotted two blips moving together about five miles north-east of us. We figured this was a tugboat pulling a barge. We then noticed another blip about three miles south-east of us, moving fast and right for us, so I went up on deck and blew the air horn, and Cody tried to call the vessel on the radio. No reply.

It was a tense time. It's eerie when you can't see anything and yet the radar tells you something is near. You keep expecting to be rammed by a huge ship zooming out of the fog. My heart was pound-pound-pounding, expecting that huge something to appear any minute.

We turned on the engine and prepared to change course if the thing got closer than two miles, but then the blip blew right past us. A little later, five more blips, but still no answer on the radio. It was scary, fearing that a big barge could plough right over you and keep going, not even knowing it had hit you.

Uncle Stew spent a lot of time flipping through manuals, and what he concluded is that since we'd been getting cloudbursts all night, our radar was probably picking up rain clouds! We felt stupid to think that we'd been blowing our horn at rain clouds and trying to call them on the radio.

Morale seems OK among the boat family today, but we don't get enough sleep. I think the reason we seem so tired – beyond not getting unbroken stretches of sleep – is that everything we do, even the simplest of actions, requires such effort. Just walking a few steps is a major production. It's like rock climbing, where you have to plot where each hand and each foot is going to go before you can actually move.

I walk at the pace of a ninety-year-old woman or

someone with broken legs. You have to brace yourself at every wave and be prepared for the shock of slamming into a wall. You can't stand freely for more than a few seconds without losing your balance from the motion of the boat.

Cooking is difficult because even though the stove is on a gimbal, which rocks around with the boat to keep the surface level, everything else flies around, spills, falls off shelves and generally makes a mess.

When you eat, you can't ever let go of your plate, and you can't drink while you eat because then you'd have to put something down, and you don't have enough hands.

Sleeping is another challenge. You keep odd hours; there's always lots of noise (things clanging about, people bumping into things, sails flapping, people talking); you sleep in a different bed every time (whichever one is empty); and there's always the threat of rolling out of your bed and having things fly off shelves and onto your head, or having a leak appear over your sleeping bag.

But still, in spite of all that, I like living on a boat. I like being this whole self-contained unit that can charge across the ocean with the wind.

Last night, in my fitful sleep, I dreamed my recurring dream, the one with The Wave. It rose up so high, towering higher, higher, a huge black wall of water, and then it curled at the top and I was a little blot beneath it and down turned The Wave and I woke up with my mouth wide open, ready to scream.

I hate that dream.

30

Knots

Learned an end-knot from Sierra-Oscar (Sophie) today. Easy! You put these little knots at the ends of the lines so they don't slip through the hole thingys and go flapping out in the water.

When I asked Sophie where she'd learned all these knots, she got this look that she sometimes gets when you ask her questions. She gazes out across the water, as if the answer might be there on the horizon. 'I dunno,' she said. She looked down at the rope between her fingers. 'Maybe someone showed me a long time ago.'

Got the radio code memorized. Beat Mr Know-it-all to it. Huh, huh, huh.

Both sun and dolphins joined us today, so it was a fine day. You can't beat sun and dolphins. Even my father came up on deck to watch the dolphins. He said, 'Makes you wish you were a fish, doesn't it?'

First time we've agreed on anything in a long, long time. You look at those dolphins and they seem so carefree. Nobody's scolding them for doing things wrong. They're just enjoying the water and their flips into the air.

While Dad was up on deck, he saw the drawings I'd made of a clove hitch and an end-knot. 'Hey,' he said, 'when did you learn how to draw?'

I could either take that as an insult, as in *I have been so unaware of you that I haven't noticed that you've been drawing for the past couple of years,* or a compliment, as in *Hey! You draw pretty well!*

I wonder which it is, insult or compliment?

31

Rosalie

A week at sea, and no one has been strangled or thrown overboard yet.

We haven't had much wind for the past few days, and fog and clouds have kept us from seeing the sun, moon and stars for much of our trip. I never realized how much I'd miss those things. I thought I'd be standing on deck out here in the middle of the ocean, gazing out into the depths of the sky, but most of what I see is grey mist.

Without sun it's hard to dry out anything, and most of our clothes are damp. We each have a secret hoard of dry T-shirts wedged into our backpacks; we guard them carefully, and pull one out only when we can't bear another minute of dampness. Ah, that dry shirt, how good it feels!

We've had animal visitors the last few days, and it surprises me how eager I am to see them. Company! Yesterday, a little black bird landed in the cockpit, looking pitiful and bedraggled. I called Cody up from the cabin to see it. 'Hey there, birdie,' he said, gently tapping its webbed feet and stroking its bill. 'Where'd you get this lump on your beak? Where'd you come from? How'd you get so wet?'

Cody warmed it in his hands and dried it against

his shirt. 'It's a cute little peep, isn't it?' Cody said. And so we started calling it Little Peep.

By the time I woke up for my next watch, Little Peep had made her way down below deck and into the cupboard next to the navigation table. Uncle Mo was sitting there drawing her portrait, and he showed me how to draw scraggly feathers. Little Peep stayed in the cupboard for a few hours, as if she liked posing.

Another bird just like Little Peep followed the boat all night and into the next day. We figured it might be Little Peep's mate, but the other bird didn't land, and Little Peep didn't seem to notice.

Cody tried putting her inside his shirt to warm her up, but I think that scared her, because she started flapping her wings. She flew shakily to the lifeline and then took off again and slowly circled the boat, not very gracefully, before taking off over the waves.

'Bye-bye, Little Peep,' Cody called.

I didn't want her to go; I could hardly bear it, seeing her all alone out there.

'You sound stupid,' Brian said, imitating Cody. 'Oh, Little Peep! Oh, Little Peep!' Brian raised his arms in the air, as if he were sending a message up to heaven. 'We are just a floating refuge for lost souls.'

Cody looked Brian up and down. 'Ain't that the truth?' he said.

Yesterday we also saw whales, little pilot whales

that look like dolphins, except that their heads are round instead of tapering into a long nose.

'Whales ahoy!' Cody shouted.

We lay flat on our stomachs on the deck watching them. The whales came close to the boat, but not as close as the dolphins, and they stayed at the stern. After a while, we could identify some of them – a mother and her baby swimming side by side, and one really huge one off to starboard.

I was hypnotized by this threesome. I decided the huge whale off to the side was the father, and he was circling around, protecting the mother and the baby. Mostly the baby whale stayed right up next to the mother, bumping into her, but occasionally the baby would veer away and wobble and look very silly, and then it would swim back to its mother and bump into her again. It seemed very important to me that they stay all together, and I felt nervous and touchy when I couldn't see all three of them.

Uncle Dock joined us. 'Most beauteous!' he said. And as we watched the whales, Uncle Dock told us the story of a woman he'd known. Her name was Rosalie and she loved whales with all her heart. She read everything there was to read about whales and she saw every movie that ever had a whale in it and she had pictures of whales on her walls and little stuffed toy whales and tiny whale figurines.

'But she'd never seen a real live whale,' Uncle Dock said, 'not up front, you know? And one day I rented a boat and took her out on the ocean, and all day long we searched for whales and all day long she prayed for whales. It was a beautiful day.'

'And did you see a whale?' I asked.

'Not that day.'

'You went again?'

'Yep. I traded my best fishing rod to the boat's owner because I was about as poor as a flea, and off we went again. All day long we searched for whales—'

'And all day long she prayed for whales—'

'That's right,' Uncle Dock said. 'And then – there – just as we were turning back to shore – there – oh it was magnificent! A pearly grey whale rose slowly up out of the water, and Rosalie – oh, Rosalie! She opened her mouth in a big wide "O" and her eyes were so big and bright and we watched that beautiful whale as he glided along, and then he disappeared back into the sea.'

Uncle Dock sighed a long, long sigh.

'And Rosalie?' I said. 'What happened to Rosalie?'

Dock stood and brushed off his trousers, as if he were brushing away the memory. 'Oh, she married somebody else.'

Cody stood and opened his arms wide and shouted out across the water, 'Rosalie! Oh, Rosalie!'

Dock smiled and joined in. 'Rosalie! Oh, Rosalie!'

Then Dock shook his head and ambled away, disappearing below deck.

Brian was watching me watch the whales. 'Sophie the Whale Girl,' he said.

'Don't you ever get interested in what's out there?' I asked him. 'Don't you think they're amazing?'

'Enh,' he said.

'Don't you think they're more interesting than books and charts?' I asked him.

'Enh,' he repeated, but he came and stood beside me and he even laughed once, when the baby whale banged into her mother, but then he seemed embarrassed to be caught enjoying himself and he retreated to his charts.

Today, more dolphins came and played in the bow waves. One of them jumped clear out of the water, right in front of the bow, as if to say, 'Watch me! Wow!'

I was fixed on a mother-and-baby pair who swam in perfect synchronization, as if they were the same being.

'The baby's like a replica of its mother,' Brian said, 'just smaller, but with all its mother's grace and speed—'

'Brian,' I said, 'are you actually getting interested in these things?'

'Look,' he said. 'It's like she's teaching it how to play,' and then he said, 'Why do you think they trust us so much?'

And that's exactly the feeling I had, that they instinctively trusted us, and really, it made me want to cry. It should have made me want to laugh, because it was as if they were inviting us to join them, be a part of their play. They seemed so overwhelmingly happy: playing, investigating, gliding and leaping and rolling. I don't know why it made me want to cry. I just kept thinking that there they were and here I was. They didn't have any burdens and they wanted to be with us, but I was way up on deck and I felt as if I weighed a ton.

Uncle Mo brought out his sketchpad and quickly, deftly, drew the dolphins leaping in the air. He said, 'They remind you of being a child, with all that curiosity and energy. They remind you that this is what you could be, not what you should grow out of.' He looked around at me and Cody and Brian, as if he'd just realized we were there, and then turned back to his drawing, mumbling, 'Or something like that.'

32

Bompie and the Swimming Hole

Fog, fog, fog, fog, fog.

And I'm talking radio code in my sleep. Hotel-Echo-Lima-Papa! (HELP!)

We've seen whales and dolphins and a little black bird. I want to be a fish or a bird. Swim in the water or fly in the air.

Sophie got really attached to the bird and worried and fretted over it. I told her she'd better watch it because she was becoming just like Uncle Stew.

'I am not!' she said.

Every time dolphins or whales come and play by the boat, Sophie is up there watching. She can't take her eyes off them, and then she starts wondering where they came from and where they're going and why they're here and if they are part of a family, if they're all related.

Brian had to get his two cents in about orphans again. First, he kept calling Little Peep *the orphan bird*, and then, when we were watching the dolphins, Brian was going on about how the baby dolphin was imitating the mother. 'I wonder what happens to orphan dolphins,' he said. 'How do they learn anything?'

Sophie said, 'I guess they're smart enough to figure it out on their own. They probably don't have a lot of choice.'

And Brian said, 'Is that what you did, figure it out on your own?'

And Sophie said, 'Look! Look at that! Did you see her leap?' and then she went below deck. When I went down a few minutes later, she was juggling pretzel packets. She's getting good.

'Show me how to juggle four things,' she said. 'Then show me how to accidentally-on-purpose bean someone and knock him overboard.'

I figure she was referring to Mr Know-it-all, Bravo-Romeo, Brian.

Later she told another Bompie story. It went like this:

Near Bompie's house out in the country was a swimming hole. It was at a bend in a creek and was very deep. Big rocks and tree limbs jutted out from the side, and you could climb out on these rocks and tree limbs and leap into the water, *whoosh!* It was a dangerous place because there were also rocks and tree limbs under the water and you couldn't always see where you might land. And because it was a dangerous place, Bompie was forbidden to swim there.

But one hot hot hot summer day, Bompie really really wanted to swim. He wanted to leap into that cool water and float there until his skin wrinkled up. So he went down to the swimming hole and climbed up on one of the rocks and stood there looking at that cool water down below. Oh, it was hot. Hot hot hot. And the water looked so cool. And so Bompie jumped.

And he hit that cool cool water and it felt so delicious and down down he went and *thunk!* He hit something – a rock? A tree? And *thunk!* He smashed against something else. And he was dizzy down there under the cool cool water and *whack!* His head banged against something hard.

And he was turning and twisting and all confused down there in the swirling cool cool water, but at last he bobbed up and he climbed out and lay on the muddy bank until his head stopped hurting, and then he went home.

'He got a whipping!' Brian said. 'Right? I bet his father gave him one huge whipping!'

'That's right,' Sophie said. 'And then—'

'Wait,' Brian said. 'Don't tell me. Apple pie, right? His mother gave him some apple pie, right?'

'No,' Sophie said.

'What?' Brian said. 'No apple pie? But didn't she want to give him some apple pie because he was safe? No apple pie?'

'No apple pie,' Sophie said. 'This time it was blueberry pie. She was out of apples.'

When she finished her story, Brian said, 'Why in the heck does Bompie keep going in the water?'

'What?' Sophie said. 'What do you mean?'

'If he always gets in trouble in the water, why does Bompie keep going *in* the water? You'd think he'd stay about as far away from water as he could get.'

Sophie's lips were pressed tightly together, and suddenly she looked so fragile to me.

I said, 'Maybe that's exactly why Bompie keeps going in the water—'

Sophie looked at me. Her eyes were bright and wet.

'Maybe,' I said, 'he's afraid of the water, but he keeps

going back to it because he has to – there's something he has to prove—'

'Like what?' Brian said.

'I don't know,' I said. 'But if you think about it – if you conquered the thing that scared you the most, then maybe you'd feel – I don't know – you'd feel free or something. You think?'

Brian said, 'Well, that's stupid. If you're afraid of something, there's probably a good reason for it, and it means you should learn to stay away from those things. That's what I think.'

Sophie didn't say anything. She went over to the railing and stood there like she does, staring out over the water.

33

Life

This morning, I woke up thinking, *I hate the sea and the sea hates me.* It was weird. I don't hate the sea.

Uncle Stew was in the galley when I went in to get something to eat. I don't see him much. He's usually sleeping when I'm awake, and I'm sleeping when he's awake. So far, that's been just fine with me.

It was awkward being in the galley with him, just the two of us. I never know what to say to him. So I decided to ask him about Rosalie.

'Did you ever meet Rosalie?' I asked. 'The Rosalie that Uncle Dock told us about?'

'Sure,' he said.

'Uncle Dock liked her a lot, right?'

'To put it mildly,' Uncle Stew said. He was fiddling with a stack of lists, crossing things out, adding new things.

'So when Rosalie married someone else, Uncle Dock must've been upset, right? He must've had his heart broken, right?'

'Something like that,' Uncle Stew said.

'So what did he do?' I asked. 'Did he just forget about her or what?'

Uncle Stew looked up. '*Forget* about Rosalie? Are you kidding? Why do you think we made all those stops – Block Island, Martha's Vineyard, Grand Manan?'

'What? Why? Wasn't Dock just visiting his friends? Weren't we just getting *The Wanderer* fixed?'

'Sure,' he said. 'Sure.' He shuffled his papers, restacking them neatly. 'Listen,' he said. 'Don't tell Dock I told you what I'm going to tell you. He's a little sensitive about Rosalie.'

'I won't tell,' I said.

'Block Island – that's where Uncle Dock first met Rosalie.'

'Really?' I said.

'And Martha's Vineyard? Remember Joey? Well, Joey is Rosalie's brother.'

'Her brother? Really?'

'And from Joey, Dock found out that after Rosalie's husband died—'

'Her husband died? She's not married any more?' I said.

'That's right,' Uncle Stew said. 'So Dock found out that Rosalie went to Grand Manan to visit Frank and to see the whales—'

'You mean our Frank – the Frank we met on Grand Manan? That Frank?'

'That's the one.'

'But Rosalie? Where was Rosalie when we were there?'

'Gone.'

'Well, where *is* she?'

'Guess,' Uncle Stew said.

But I couldn't guess then, because Uncle Dock came below, and Uncle Stew got very busy with his papers and made it clear that the subject was closed.

I tried to ask Uncle Stew later, but he said, 'I told you too much. Better let it be for now.'

I said, 'You sure know a lot about Rosalie. I thought nobody ever told you anything.'

'Huh, huh, huh,' he said. 'I still know a few things.'

And so I've been wondering where Rosalie is, and maybe we're not really going to Bompie. Maybe Uncle Dock is taking us somewhere else, in search of Rosalie. Maybe she's in Greenland; I think that's on the way. Or maybe she's right back in the United States and Dock is going to decide he has to turn around and go find her.

Uncle Dock worried me last night when I was on watch with him. I was steering, and he was standing on the foredeck, staring out at the sea. He turned around and looked at me, studying me for a minute, and then he said, 'What's it all about, Sophie?'

'How do you mean? What's *what* all about?'

He sighed a heavy sigh. 'You know. Life.'

'You're asking *me*?' I said.

His lower lip puckered under his upper lip. I thought he was going to cry, and this would be shocking, because Uncle Dock is always such a steady, calm sort of person. You don't expect him to be worrying about what life is, and you certainly don't expect him to cry in the middle of the night on a sailboat.

But then he strolled back to the aft deck and started puttering with some lines, and that's all he said about life. I stared out at the water and up at the sky and had the strangest rush of feelings. First I was completely peaceful, as if this was the most perfect place on earth to be, and then suddenly the peacefulness turned into wide, wide loneliness.

And so I started thinking about life insurance and how nice it would be if you could get insurance that your life would be happy, and that everyone you knew could be happy, and they could all do what they really wanted to do, and they could all find the people they wanted to find.

34

Little Kid Nightmares

I haven't had much sleep because my father's been badgering me, and Uncle Stew and Brian were arguing, and Uncle Dock yelled at me for leaving a line lying loose on deck, and it's been raining and foggy, and the sea's been heaving and things keep crashing on my head.

When I do finally sleep, Sophie wakes me, screaming, because she's having nightmares, but she won't say what they're about. One time she told me about that little kid she knows.

When the little kid was maybe three years old, the little kid went to the ocean. Maybe the little kid's mother was along too, but Sophie wasn't quite sure about that. The little kid lay down on a blanket (it was blue, Sophie said) and fell asleep.

Then there was water, water pouring over the little kid; it looked like a huge black wall of water. The little kid's mother grabbed the little kid's hand, but the water wanted the little kid and was pulling, pulling, and the little kid couldn't see and couldn't breathe.

Whish! The little kid's mother yanked the little kid upright.

'You know what, though?' Sophie said. 'That little kid still dreams about a wave coming.'

'You mean that little kid is still afraid of the water?'

'I didn't say that,' Sophie said. 'The little kid loves the water, loves the ocean—'

'But why does the little kid keep having that dream?'

'I don't know,' Sophie said. 'Maybe it was something about the unexpectedness of it, the being safe and sound asleep and warm and happy, and then that wave sneaking up and trying to take the little kid away—'

'Wow,' I said. 'It's as if the wave is haunting the little kid, like the little kid is afraid that the wave will come back—'

'Maybe,' Sophie said. 'Or maybe not—'

All day long, Sophie acted weird. She'd stare out at the water and then rush below deck and then she'd rush back up, as if she was suffocating down below, and up and down she went, up and down. Maybe she was worrying about the little kid.

35

The Blue Bopper

We've been at sea for a week and a half now, and *The Wanderer* has travelled over 1,300 miles. We are over halfway there, halfway to Bompie! We've gone through two time zones, so that our clocks are now two hours ahead of what they were when we left. There are three more time zones ahead. Each time we change the clocks, Cody says, 'Bye-bye, hour!' Where do those hours go?

We're about 500 miles east of Newfoundland, and 900 miles south of Greenland. I keep expecting Uncle Dock to say, 'Hey, let's stop in Greenland!' or 'Let's stop in Newfoundland!' and then we'd stop and he'd go off hunting for Rosalie. But so far, there's been no mention of stopping.

It's been very cold the last few days, but it's warming up as we near the Gulf Stream. Uncle Stew says the combination of the Labrador Current (the coldest current in the Atlantic, coming from the north) and the Gulf Stream (the warmest current, coming from the south) makes for 'very interesting weather patterns.'

'Which means what?' I asked.

'Oh, you know, sudden storms, violent storms—'

I can't tell whether Uncle Stew is testing me when he says things like this – trying to see if I will get scared and cry – or whether he says these things to prepare me for what might come.

I'm not going to show if I'm scared, and I'm not going to cry.

Yesterday, when we came on the edge of a thunderstorm, Uncle Stew went into a flurry of shouting orders. 'Turn off the electrics!'

'Why?' Cody and I asked.

'Do you want to be a humongous lightning rod?'

Massive dark clouds hovered in the distance and a surge of wind whipped *The Wanderer.*

Uncle Stew rattled off a list: 'Radar!'

Cody flipped it off. 'Checkerino.'

'GPS!'

'Off-erino!'

'Loran!'

'Zap-o!'

Uncle Stew shouted at Cody. 'What the heck are you saying? Are they off or not?'

'Off-erino!' Cody said.

I didn't stay to hear the end of it, because I was on watch. We were racing along and it felt so terrific, all that wind! We had our foul-weather gear on, so we didn't mind the torrents of rain beating down as we ploughed through the water. It felt as if we should have some loud, dramatic classical music sounding in the background. You feel as if every inch of you is alive and you are working hard to *stay* alive and the boat is helping you and you are helping it and everyone is in there together, and *whoosh*, away you go!

We've been making contact with civilization nearly every night, and Cody has surprised everyone by becoming the ham radio king. There's a ton of lingo involved, and you have to be on your toes at all times to know what's going on. Our call number is N1IQB Maritime Mobile, and in ham radio lingo, you say it like this: November One India Quebec Bravo Maritime Mobile. It's really cool to listen to Cody talking in what sounds like a foreign language:

'This is N1IQB Maritime Mobile . . . November One India Quebec Bravo Maritime Mobile . . . Over.'

Uncle Mo taught us these new bits today. It's more code-talk:

QSL = Do you copy?

88 = Hugs and kisses.

So here's Cody on the radio:

Cody: 'Roger, this is N1IQB Maritime Mobile trying to get in touch with WB2YPZ Maritime Mobile, Whiskey Bravo Two Yankee Papa Zulu, over.'

Ham net: 'Roger, N1IQB, send your traffic, over.'

We haven't been able to get through to anyone we know yet, so we have to ask at the net for somebody in Connecticut we can leave a message with or make a phone call through. Cody says most ham operators on land can make a phone patch; they hook their phone up to their radio, make a reverse charge call to the number and then you can talk to whoever you want by phone.

The voices are distorted and unclear, but it's like a miracle when it works, which has not been very often. We've tried to get through to my father, but without any luck.

When Cody is working the radio, I get so excited. You really want to hear a familiar voice! But then as time goes on and you can't get a connection or you can't hear well, it makes me so annoyed that I wish we weren't even trying. And it still feels as if we are cheating by being able to contact other people.

I said as much to Uncle Dock, and he said, 'What? You *want* to be cut off from everybody else? From the world?'

'I didn't say that. It's just that we're supposed to be doing this on our own.'

Uncle Dock said, 'Sophie, it's not a bad thing to rely on other people, you know.'

I've been thinking about that all day. I don't know why it is that it seems important for me to be able to do everything myself and not rely on anyone else. I'd always thought that was a good way to be, but Uncle Dock made it sound selfish. I don't get it.

At lunch today, one of those rare occasions when we all happened to be awake at the same time, Uncle Dock said, 'Hey, remember the time we found that rubber dinghy? You know, when we were kids—'

Uncle Mo said, 'Yeah! The blue one?'

Uncle Stew chimed in, 'Hey, I remember that! It

was washed up on shore, right? And we claimed it as our own—'

'And we named it – remember what we named it?' Uncle Dock said.

Mo and Stew thought about that a while. Then Stew got a huge smile on his face – maybe the first smile I've seen on that face – and said, 'I know! *The Blue Bopper*! *The Blue Bopper*, right?'

Mo laughed. 'Yeah! *The Blue Bopper*!'

'And remember,' Stew said, 'how we were so excited to get in it and we pushed it out into the waves and we were laughing like hyenas—'

'And we were laughing so hard that we didn't even notice—'

'That we were being pulled out farther and farther—'

Stew was choking by now, he was laughing so hard. 'And – then we realized—'

'We didn't have any paddles!'

They were all laughing by this time. At first I was laughing too, because *they* were laughing – it was very funny to see them all acting so goofy. But then I couldn't figure out what was so funny about them being in a dinghy without paddles, and it gave me goosebumps, thinking of them floating, floating, helpless.

'So what happened?' Cody asked. 'How'd you get back?'

'Hmm,' Uncle Mo said. 'Don't really remember that part.'

'But we got back somehow,' Uncle Stew said.

Of course I should have known that they all got

back safely, because here they were telling the story, but somehow it wasn't until Uncle Stew said that they got back that I felt this huge wave of relief slide over me.

'And then Bompie – oh boy!' Uncle Dock said.

'What?' Cody asked. 'Did he give you a whipping?'

'Bompie?' Uncle Stew said. 'Bompie never laid a hand on us in his entire life.'

'That's right,' Uncle Dock agreed.

'So what did Bompie do when you got back?' Cody asked.

Uncle Stew said, 'He took us out to the shed and said, "See these here wooden things? These wooden things are called paddles. You might want to take a couple of these here paddles next time you go out on that ocean." '

It sounded pretty funny the way Uncle Stew told it, and they sat around on deck laughing a long time. I had to go down below because I couldn't get that image out of my head, of them floating out in the ocean in the dinghy without any paddles.

I went up the mast again yesterday, this time to the very top! The flag line broke and was stuck in the block at the top of the mast, so I tied a new line to my harness and Cody pulled me up. The boat dipped and rolled and the wind raged, and it was all I could do to hang on. It was like a test between me and the wind, as if the wind were saying, *Can you do it, Sophie? Bet you can't!* And as if I were saying, *I can do this! Watch me!* The hard things sometimes turn out to make you feel the best.

We also noticed cracks in the ends of the booms, where they come together. This is a big problem. Uncle Dock says we will lash-and-tongue them and hope that the cracks don't get any bigger.

Also on the big problem list is the water maker – that broke too. Nobody's really sure exactly what the problem is, but Brian is determined to take a hot shower tonight, so we'll power through and try to fix it. And speaking of showers, we all stink! Everything on the boat stinks too.

Uncle Stew is yelling at me to help him fix something, so I guess this is over and out from Sophie: Sierra-Oscar-Papa-Hotel-India-Echo.

QSL?

88.

V

Wind and Waves

36

Bouncing

Rolling and bouncing and wanting to puke.

Later:

Puking.

Later:

Not puking.

37

Wind

The sea, the sea, the sea. It heaves and rolls and rumbles at me.

The winds have been howling since last night at sunset, and we've nearly worn ourselves out coping. When the wind first picked up, we reefed the main, pulling it down and tying the bottom to itself to make the sail smaller, and we were about to reef the mizzen when the main boom broke. We'd been fearing that would happen.

Uncle Dock and Uncle Mo lashed the ends together with line, torqued it with a steel pipe and then lashed the pipe to the boom. We're praying it holds.

The wind howls around the sails, lunging at us from one side and then careening around the other, knocking us off our feet. The waves swell and grow, blowing streaks of foam. I don't know how to judge how high they are – they seem two storeys high – and you can't believe it's water standing up like that, arching over you.

We've now double-reefed both sails and Uncle Dock is barking orders in true captain fashion. I'm glad I know what most of the terms mean. You don't have time to think about where starboard is or where the bosun's locker is or what the difference is between a halyard and an outhaul; you have to know. And I'm glad that I've touched every line and pulley on *The Wanderer* and know how things work, because I feel as if I'm really helping and right now it doesn't matter if it's a girl or a boy doing it, as long as somebody gets it done.

Dock is calling—

38

Howling

It's all wind and walls of water. Everything howls and churns. I think we are doomed.

39

Bobbing

We've lashed down every loose thing and have been powering through for about six hours, but the wind is still increasing and is clocking around from the south-east. Earlier, it was as if we were riding a roller coaster and sometimes it was almost fun, racing along, trying to stay perpendicular to the waves so they wouldn't push us over. Shooting up the wave, shooting down it, up and down!

Now the waves are more fierce, cresting and toppling over, like leering drooling monsters spewing heavy streaks of foam through the air. Sometimes as the big waves rear up behind you, you can see huge fish suspended in them.

It's so hard to see, so hard to think, so hard to stay upright. I was kneeling on deck, fastening a line, and when I turned back, I couldn't see anyone else on deck, even though just a minute before I'd seen Dock and Cody and Uncle Mo there, and when I shouted out to them the wind blew my voice back into my mouth. Inside my head I heard a little voice whimpering.

'Too much tension on the sails!' Uncle Dock roared, as he emerged from the mist. He was staring up at the sails, where grommets at the top of both sails were popping out, *zing, snap, zing!* The main was ripping all along the top of the sail.

We got it down and tried to put up the heavy-duty storm trysail, but before it was all the way up, half the grommets had torn out. A blast of wind pushed Uncle Mo up against me, flattening me against the jackstays.

'Flag line on the mizzen broke!' Cody shouted.

'See?' Uncle Mo said, as he tried to stand up. 'That boy's no idjit. He knows a few things.'

The mizzen sail also started ripping, so we brought that one down too, but as we brought it down, the halyard vibrated free and stuck at the top of the mast.

Uncle Dock clung to the rail and said to the sea, 'Oh, Rosalie!'

And here we are, bare-masted in gale winds and high seas, bobbing like a cork, about as far from land as we could possibly be.

40

No Time

No time for stories of Bompie, for juggling, for learning knots. The wind howls and the seas rage and our sails are down.

When I came below my father hugged me.

'I don't want to die,' I told him.

He held on to me. 'You can't die,' he said. 'You can't. And Sophie can't die like this.'

'Sophie can't? What about Uncle Dock – and Brian – and—'

'We can't let it happen.'

What does he mean? It's as if he is talking in code. It's as if everyone talks in code where Sophie is concerned. Even Sophie talks in code.

41

Surfing

I've been at the helm for much of the time, and those waves have no mercy. Walls of water come crashing over us every five minutes, and the wind howls – *Hooo-rrrrrr! Hooo-rrrrr!* – and tries to blow us over. One monstrous wave swept Cody right off his feet as he was working up on the bow.

'Get that safety harness on, Cody!' Uncle Dock barked. 'Lock down that wheel, Sophie!'

I locked it down as close to our heading as I could, while Uncle Stew made some hot chocolate to warm us, and we all gathered round to try and figure out what to do next. We are bone-tired from battling the wind and waves. There is so much power and force in the wind and water. We're like wee grains of sand out here, surrounded by tremendous energy that could pulverize us into a zillion atoms. You can't help but feel that the wind and the water have something against you personally.

I'm sitting in the forward cabin, and the waves are slightly bigger than before, with the wind blowing at fifty knots. The sea looks white and eerie, and there is an odd smell in the air, like fish and seaweed and mould all mixed together.

Uncle Stew and Brian are trying to fix the trysail,

but the wind has shifted again and we are making our course without any sails at all. We are no longer beating against the waves; instead, they are pushing us along at great speed.

Cody just shouted down that the mizzen boom has broken too.

What next?

Later:

We've decided not to raise the storm sail because of our limited halyards and the stress on the booms. Instead, we are surfing. Surfing to Ireland.

Later:

I'm in a funk, even though I don't want to be. It's that same old thing that bugs me from time to time. I want to do all the gnarly work on the boat, like all the stuff on deck, and I keep volunteering to do it, but I always seem to get stuck at the helm.

'Don't think you can handle that, Sophie. Take the helm.'

'A bit rough up there, Sophie. Take the helm.'

There's nothing wrong with being at the wheel; it's just that it looks so exciting up there, out in the open, with the boat flying and the waves crashing.

Later:

When I volunteered to help put up the trysail, Dock asked Cody instead, and I threw a little fit.

'I know I'm not as strong as Cody, but I make up for it in effort!' I shouted.

Uncle Dock looked weary. 'Take the helm, Sophie,' he said.

I was standing there at the wheel having my own personal, angry, silent talk into the wind when Brian came up to me and said, 'Quit being so selfish, Sophie.'

'Selfish? Me? What the heck are you talking about?' I was so angry at him. I don't know where it came from.

'This isn't all about you, you know. Everybody should do what he does best, and everybody's got to take orders from the captain.' He jabbed his hand at my shoulder.

'Quit it!'

He jabbed me again. 'You're only on this trip because Dock took pity on you. You're only here because you're an—'

'What? I'm what?'

The boat rolled and he pushed his hand at me and I pushed him back and he went up against the rail. The boat rolled again and he was struggling to get upright and grab the rail. He was going over, and I was frozen, clutching the wheel.

Cody appeared out of nowhere and grabbed Brian, pushed him towards the centre of the boat, and said, 'Put your stupid harness on, Mr Know-it-all!'

Brian dived into the cabin, and Cody gave me an odd look. 'What was that all about?'

'Nothing,' I said. I was shaking, and I'm still

shaking, and Brian is avoiding me, and I'm avoiding him.

I don't feel like Sophie. I feel like a stupid little sea flea.

42

Battling

Ferocious wind and waves. It feels like we're in a battle, and it's better when you're up on deck trying to fix things and trying to stay upright, because when you stop and come below and have a minute to think, you know you are going to die.

Which is why I'm going back on deck.

43

Weary

It's very bad out there. We're so weary, too weary to write.

Everyone has cried today, except me. I'm not going to cry.

44

The Son

Today my father told me I'd been a good son and he'd been a bad father, and he was sorry about that.

But he was wrong: I haven't been a good son.

45

Alone

Bad, bad, bad, bad. How long can this go on?

Earlier, when I was at the helm and we all happened to be up on deck at the same time, I turned to see Uncle Stew with his arm around Brian, and Uncle Mo with his arm around Cody, and Uncle Dock gripping the rail and staring out to sea. Was he thinking of Rosalie? I wanted to leave the helm and put my arm around Uncle Dock, or have him put his arm around me, but I couldn't leave my position.

We are all alone out here.

46

Bompie at the Ocean

Maybe we have entered some weird place where the seas always rage and the wind always howls, and maybe we are going in circles and will never escape and eventually we will die of hunger.

Earlier today when Sophie and I were collapsed on bunks, trying to make ourselves sleep, she told me another Bompie story. It went like this:

When Bompie was a young man he set out for the ocean because he had never seen the ocean before. He hitch-hiked from Kentucky to the Virginia shore and when he got to the ocean he sat down in the sand and fell in love with the ocean. He loved everything about it: the smell, the sounds, the feel of the air on his face.

He waded out into the water, where the waves kept knocking him down, but still he kept going, until he was standing neck-deep, and he floated on his back staring up at the sky, and he was reminded of another ocean, far away, one in England. And he realized he *had* seen the ocean before, long ago, when he was small. And then he realized that this was the same ocean, that all that water stretched thousands of miles from Virginia to England, and maybe this water that was holding him up had once licked the shores of England and maybe it was the same water he had splashed in as a toddler.

And finally he let his feet drift downward, but he couldn't touch bottom, and he looked towards the shore and realized he'd been pulled far far away from it, and he started swimming, '*Giddy-up, giddy-up*,' he told himself, but it was so far, and he was so tired, and a wave swept over him and pushed him under, and he was so very weary, bone-weary, and he didn't know if he had enough strength to keep going, and he tried floating again, and resting and then swimming some more, and eventually he made it back to shore.

He lay down on the sand and slept, and when he woke, he hitch-hiked back to Kentucky.

You know the rest: a whipping and some pie (apples again).

47

Force Ten

The sea, the sea, the sea. It rolls and boils. It feels as if *The Wanderer* will be swallowed up, and I'm afraid.

We're in a force-ten gale, Uncle Dock says, with winds at fifty knots an hour and waves like walls of water pounding us day and night, and still we have no sails up. Every twenty minutes a wave breaks behind us and fills the cockpit with water. We all keep saying that the wind has to die down soon; it's been blowing too hard for too long.

' "Courage!" ' Uncle Dock yelled out earlier. ' "This mounting wave will roll us shoreward soon!" ' It seemed like a strange thing for him to say, since we were nowhere near shore, but then he explained that he was quoting from a poet named Tennyson.

Uncle Stew (I-Never-Get-Seasick Stew) is seasick. He looks yellow and frail, and the rest of us are covering his shifts and praying that we do not succumb too.

It's now one a.m., a wave has just filled the cockpit, and I'm up on watch. Please let the wind die down.

48

Night

Will someone find this dog-log floating in the sea? Will my mother know what happened to us?

We tried to get a message to you last night, Mom. We love you.

If I could start my life over—

There is no day. It's all night.

We have to yell to hear each other above the wind, but what I want to do is whisper. I want to say nicer things, but there is no time. All our time is spent fighting the wind.

Last night I dreamed about Sophie, and this morning I asked Uncle Dock if Sophie knew what had happened to her parents. He said, 'At some level, Sophie must know. But consciously? That's something only Sophie can answer.'

I asked him why no one would talk about it, why they wouldn't tell me or Brian. He said, 'It's not the time right now. And maybe it should come from Sophie. It's her story.'

49

Spinning

Cody and Uncle Dock and I went on watch at about one in the morning. It seemed as if the weather had started to let up, and we were hoping that by the end of our watch, we'd be able to turn *The Wanderer* over to Uncle Mo and Brian and Uncle Stew in calmer seas.

' "Smite the sounding furrows!" ' Uncle Dock yelled.

'More poetry?' I said.

'Yep,' he said.

We'd been on watch about an hour when Cody shouted to me: 'Sierra-Oscar! Your Highness – where is it?'

My head was so numb. My ears were plugged. What was he saying?

He shouted again, tugging at his belt. 'Your Highness!'

I tapped my head, as if there were a crown there, and curtsied. I thought he was playing some kind of game.

He left his post and dashed below deck, and when he came up, he was holding my safety harness. Oh. He'd been saying *harness*. I felt so stupid. Cody fastened it for me and said, 'You've got to wear this, Sophie. You've got to.'

'Aw,' I said, 'weather's letting up; we're OK.'

'We're not OK, Sophie. Wear this.'

But the seas did seem to settle for an hour or so, and the wind eased. I watched Cody as he moved about the deck. One minute he was trimming a sail; the next minute he was fastening a line, scooping up a loose cushion, stowing it, returning to the sails. Dock was doing the same things on the other side of the deck. They moved with seeming ease in those choppy seas, and it seemed as if this were a play and their movements were gracefully choreographed.

Around three-thirty in the morning, about a half hour before the end of our watch, the wind and waves picked up again. Uncle Dock was in the cockpit, Cody was at the wheel, and I was sitting next to the hatch that covers the cabin, watching the waves coming up behind us, in order to warn Cody and Dock when a big one was on its way.

As each wave started to build, it made me weak and queasy, not so much from the motion, but from the fear that this wave would be too big, that this one would roll us over. Off in the distance, I saw a wave that looked different from all the others. It was much bigger, at least fifty feet high it seemed, and not dark like the others. It was white – all white – and the entire wave was foam, as if it had just broken. I stared at it for a couple of seconds, trying to figure out what was up with it, and by that time it was right behind us, growing bigger and bigger, still covered with foam.

I shouted a warning to Cody: 'Cody! Look behind—'

He turned, looked quickly and then turned back around, crouched down and braced himself.

Most of the waves that break behind us roll under the stern, the foam sometimes coming up over the sides of the cockpit. But this wave was unlike any other. It had a curl, a distinct high curl. I watched it growing up behind us, higher and higher, and then it curled over *The Wanderer*, thousands of gallons of water, white and lashing.

'Cody! Dock!' I yelled.

And then I saw it hit Cody like a million bricks on his head and shoulders. I took a deep breath, closed my eyes and covered my head.

I was inside the wave, floating, spinning, thrown this way and that. I remember thinking *Hold that breath, Sophie*, and then wondering if my breath would last. Such intense force was pushing me; it didn't seem like it could possibly be water – soft, gentle water – that was doing this.

I couldn't remember about the harness. I didn't feel attached to anything. Was it on or not?

I was going overboard; I was sure of it. Underwater forever, twisting and turning, scrunched in a little ball. Was this the ocean? Was I over the side and in the sea? Was I four years old? In my head, a child's voice was screaming, 'Mommy! Daddy!'

And then I heard, 'Sophie!'

I think I will be sick now, writing about it.

50

The Wave

The Wave. The Wave. It blew me straight through the canvas dodger which covers the cabin, and onto the deck next to the rail. I was on my back, like a turtle, arms and legs flailing for something to grab on to. My first instinct was to do whatever it took to get out of there before another wave hit. My harness was on and it had held; if it hadn't, I would have been far behind the boat by then.

I saw Uncle Stew, with his yellow face sticking out of the main hatch. He looked like someone had just punched him in the stomach. His mouth was hanging open and he was staring straight ahead.

All I could think of was *Where are Cody and Uncle Dock?*

Uncle Stew grabbed at my harness and pulled me back through the dodger hole and down the hatch. Below, I slumped onto the navigation table. My legs were killing me. I thought they were both broken. I felt sick and battered and my heart seemed to be beating faster than my body knew how to keep up, and my legs couldn't hold me even though I was sitting down.

I slid onto the floor in at least a foot of water, trying to focus on where people were and if everyone was still on board and if everyone was OK. There were clothes and bits of food sloshing around. There was Uncle Stew. And Uncle Mo. Brian. My brain couldn't count, couldn't focus.

I crawled across the floor. Who was missing? Stew. Mo. Brian. They were all here. I was scrabbling across the floor through the water and the sloshing crud. And then I was screaming, 'Cody Dock Cody Dock!' I made it to the aft cabin and collapsed on top of a pile of wet clothes. 'Cody Dock Cody Dock!'

And then Brian was there, kneeling beside me. 'He's OK, Sophie. He's OK. He's up top.'

'Who's up top?'

'Dock. He's OK.'

'But Cody? Where's Cody?'

There was a blur of people racing to and fro, scrambling to pump out the water.

'He's OK, Sophie,' Brian said. 'He's here. I saw him.'

'What happened to your arm? It looks funny.'

Brian cradled his right arm in his left. 'Banged it, I guess.'

My brain kept insisting on making sure everyone was there. I must have gone through everyone's name twenty times, and each time I'd tell myself where each person was: Dock: he's working the emergency bilge pump. Mo: he's on deck, securing the hatch. Brian: he's bailing down here. Stew: he's bailing too. Cody? Where's Cody? Where's Cody? I always got stuck on Cody. Then I'd figure it out: he's on deck.

And then there was Cody standing at the bottom of the ladder, his face covered in blood. The force of The Wave had blown his head right into the wheel, gashing open his nose and left eyebrow. He rushed past me into the bathroom.

I followed him and found him sitting on the floor with a bunch of plasters on his lap, looking helpless and confused.

'Sophie?' he said. 'Fix me.'

I crawled to the forecabin to get the emergency medical bag and crawled back to Cody and started on his face, cleaning the blood off with fresh water. The gashes were deep, and when I began cleaning them with antiseptic, he winced and started vomiting.

I was babbling, 'It's OK, Cody, it's OK, it's the shock, it's OK, Cody.'

I recleaned the gashes and put loads of gauze over his wounds and taped him up good. He looked pretty wretched, but his face was temporarily salvaged. I found him some dry clothes and helped him onto a bunk and covered him with wool blankets.

Pain darts are shooting up and down my legs while I'm sitting here next to Cody, keeping watch over him. All around me is the most appalling mess. The canvas dodger is lying halfway up the deck, and its metal frame, which had been bolted onto the deck, has been ripped out. The table in the cockpit is broken, our ham radio antenna gone, the hatch doors gone. The outdoor speakers are also gone, along with the bucket, a blue chair and a bunch of cushions.

The top of the emergency fresh water container was blown off and the contents sucked out. The wood in the cockpit seems about three shades lighter now, scratched and gashed.

Down below, everything is soaked. Water came in through the hatch like water out of a fire hose, gunning everything in sight. A huge pot of chilli, which was half full before The Wave hit, now is still half full, but the chilli was blown right out of the pot and replaced by salt water.

The GPS, ham radio and radar are all shot, and the kerosene heater is smashed.

It feels as if we're riding a bull, being slammed violently by every wave, hard, like rock against rock.

51

Limping

We're limping along by the seat of our pants. I feel completely out of it, like I'm not really here – as if I'm somewhere else and watching this strange movie. If I knew the ending it would help. If we are going to make it to land again, then I could relax, but if we aren't going to make it, why are we wasting all these hours fixing things and talking boat-talk? Why aren't we doing something important? But what would that be?

52

Jumbled

The sea, the sea, the sea. It thunders and rolls and unsettles me; it unsettles all of us.

We tremble as we listen to the waves pounding. When I close my eyes, all I see is that huge white wave, and all I hear is the low rumbling that grows louder and louder as the wave breaks. We are all afraid to sleep, all afraid that The Wave will return.

When we do lie down, we jolt out of bed at the slightest rumble of a new wave. I keep running through the scene in my head, over and over, from all different angles. It was like being born: I was in my rolling little world until a huge surge of water broke on me, scrunching me into a tight, round bundle and pushing me through a small space and then I was helpless and wet on my back, attached only by a small red line until a big hand pulled me away. I couldn't talk, only whimper and moan.

The hatch is secured, most of the water pumped out from below. Cody is up and at it again, but now Uncle Mo has succumbed to seasickness and so he and Uncle Stew are awfully miserable. Brian's arm is badly sprained, and Uncle Dock wrenched his back. We're a sad-looking group.

My right leg is still throbbing and hurts all around my knee and down the back of my thigh. My other leg is fine except for a sprained and sore ankle. But besides that and a big bump on the back of my head, I am in one piece physically.

Inside, though, I am in many pieces. I feel strange and raw and all jumbled up. Sometimes I feel as if one little roll of the boat or one quick movement will shatter me into a zillion pieces and all those pieces will go flinging off into the sea.

Nearby is my safety harness, that little stainless steel clip that saved my life, and one just like it saved Dock and Cody. So far.

Cody's face is still a mess. Yesterday, when he finally started to wake up, he asked me if I'd made him any pie. I didn't get it at first, but then he said, 'You know, like Bompie. He always got some apple pie when he survived something.'

'He also got a whipping,' I said, and I thought Cody would laugh at that, but instead he said, 'Do you think his father was ever sorry for those whippings?' So I told him another story about Bompie, which didn't exactly answer the question, but it seemed to fit somehow.

53

Bompie and His Father

When I was out of it after my head got bashed, Sophie told me another Bompie story. It wasn't like the others. Bompie didn't fall in the water or anything. It went like this:

When Bompie's father was very old and very sick, Bompie went to see him. Bompie sat by his father's bed every day for three weeks.

During the first week, Bompie sat there being mad at his father and was hardly able to talk to him. The second week, Bompie was even madder and he sat there reminding his father of all the times his father had whipped him.

'Remember when I fell off that bridge and nearly drowned in the Ohio River? Remember that whipping you gave me?' Bompie asked. 'And remember when I was in the car that flipped over in the river and when I came home, you whipped me black and blue?' On and on Bompie went, while his father just lay there blinking back at him.

During the third week, Bompie stopped talking and just looked at his father. He looked at his hands and his feet, his arms and his legs, his face. He touched his father's forehead and his cheeks. Then Bompie left the hospital and when he came back the next day, he said to his father, 'Look what I brought you. An apple pie!'

And his father cried and Bompie cried.

When Sophie finished Bompie's story, I wanted to give her a story too. But I couldn't think of one to tell.

54

Mr Fix-it

Although Cody's face looks bad, the rest of him seems OK, physically, that is. He's sober and serious, though, and seems to feel he has to make up for lost time. He's like a one-man Mr Fix-it, very focused on exactly what needs repairing and how to do it.

The rest of us are only able to function in short bursts, but Cody doesn't stop, not even to sleep. Everyone wants either Cody or me at the helm because we seem to have found a way to keep the boat in tune with the waves, and they say *The Wanderer* rides more smoothly when we guide her. I can't stand there very long, though, because of my legs hurting so bad.

Everyone is grateful for Cody right now. I haven't heard anyone say that out loud, but I know it's true. Maybe they are even a little grateful for me too, but it no longer seems important to worry about that.

Uncle Dock has confirmed that the GPS, ham radio and radar are all shot. We don't know where we are, and no one else knows where we are and we can't summon help if we get really desperate.

We are still without sails, praying for the wind and seas to calm, and in the meantime, we spend all our waking moments and energy cleaning up the mess. We are all quieter than usual, thinking about being alive and how fragile a line there is between being alive and not being alive.

55

Wet

Wet, wet, wet. Nearly everything is soaked. Only the fore-cabin is partly dry, so we smoosh in there when we can grab a few hours to sleep.

Sophie's leg still has pain darts shooting up and down it, but she can walk. She's very jittery, but she's trying hard to make it seem as if she has it all under control.

We're all tired, tired, tired. 'Poop-de-dooped! Huh, huh, huh,' Brian said a few minutes ago, with a little attempt at humour.

But we do have sails again and are up and running. Sophie and I double-reefed the mainsail, and got the fixed storm trysail on the mizzen. *The Wanderer* looks a bit odd, but we're moving, and we've been working hard to make the boat liveable again. The canvas dodger is back in place, the heater is repaired and the wheel (bent from my head smashing into it) is fixed.

We might make it.

56

Useful

We've been trying to use the sextant for navigation, since our GPS is 'toast', as Uncle Dock says. Brian and Uncle Stew are the only ones any good with the sextant, and I heard Cody say to them, 'Sure glad you guys know how to work that thing.'

They both looked up at Cody and smiled. They didn't even say anything snotty to him.

Cody came and sat next to me. 'You know,' he said, 'maybe that's all anybody wants, is to be useful.' He tied end-knots in each of my shoelaces. 'And have somebody else notice it,' he added.

'You're useful, Cody,' I said.

'So are you, Sierra-Oscar,' he said.

I've had a lot of trouble being on watch ever since The Wave. The waves aren't nearly as big now, but it's just too frightening. I'm always looking behind me, convinced that every wave with the slightest bit of foam on it is going to be a reincarnation of The Wave.

It seems a hundred years ago that we were lobstering and clamming on Grand Manan and trekking around Wood Island, and it seems a hundred years ago that we were eager to get under way, oblivious to what lay in wait for us.

I feel as if I have to start all over to love sailing again, because I don't love it now. I just want to get to Bompie and forget about the ocean for a while.

But we're not there yet. We're here.

I feel as if there were things inside me that were safely tucked away, sort of like the bilge down there, hidden under the floorboards of *The Wanderer*. But it feels as if the boards were blown off by The Wave and things are floating around and I don't know where to put them.

Brilliant Cody spotted and contacted a Canadian warship, which verified our position. We're near the shipping lanes now, so if we can spot at least one ship a day, Cody will be able to call them on the VHF radio and ask for their position.

We're 500 miles from Ireland, less than a week away, with luck, and then on to England.

Oh, Bompie!

57

Thinking

I am thinking about Bompie. At last I will see Bompie. Why am I scared?

58

Little Kid: Push and Pull

When I sleep, I dream of Sophie. In the dreams, she is talking in radio code and I am trying to transcribe what she is saying, but the words I write down make no sense. She talks louder and I write faster, but still I can't make sense of the words I'm putting on the page.

Yesterday, Sophie told me another story, but this one was not a Bompie story. I'd asked her if she could remember things from when she was little.

She said, 'Why do people always ask that?' And then, when I thought she was going to turn around and leave, she started telling me about the little kid again. She told it like this:

There's a little kid. And the little kid doesn't know what is going on. The little kid is just cold or hungry or scared and wants Mommy and Daddy. And when other people tell the little kid that Mommy and Daddy have gone to heaven, which is such a beautiful place, all warm and sunny with no troubles and no woes, the little kid feels bad and wonders why they didn't take their little kid with them to that beautiful place.

And everywhere the little kid goes, people ask what the little kid remembers about the grown-ups who have gone away to the beautiful place, but the little kid doesn't want to remember that painful thing. The little kid has enough to deal with every day. The little kid wants to be right here, right now, and wants to look at now and at things ahead, on that horizon over there, not back at those times the little kid got left behind.

But no matter what the little kid might want, something inside pushes the little kid ahead while something or someone pulls the little kid back.

When Sophie finished, I didn't know what to say. All I could think of was, 'Don't you wish we had some pie?'

She said, 'Yes.'

She's been very quiet ever since, as if she is listening to something or someone only she can hear. And at other times, she stands very close to me, as if she is hoping I will speak for her. Then I feel as if I am in my dream again, because I don't know what words she wants me to say for her.

59

New Dreams

You can tell that Uncle Mo is trying to be nicer to Cody. He's not barking at him any more, and he's not calling him a knuckleheaded doofus. Cody doesn't seem to know how to take this. He stares at his father, as if he is studying him.

Cody's face is looking much better. We found the adhesive sutures and were better able to close up the cuts on his eye and nose. When we get to England, Cody can go to a real doctor and get checked out. Uncle Stew says Brian should get his arm looked at, and I should get my leg checked too, but my leg is a lot better, not as sore, with only one nasty bruise left around my knee.

It's a funny thing about Uncle Stew. Now, when you'd think he'd have so many more things to worry about, he seems calmer and kinder.

When Uncle Stew was asking me about my leg, he said, 'It's odd being a parent. You feel responsible for everything, and you're so protective of your children and so worried about them that you can hardly think straight sometimes. But then sometimes you realize that you don't have control over a lot of things and sometimes you have to just hope that everything will be OK.'

He glanced over at Brian, who was tacking up a list in the galley. 'And sometimes,' Uncle Stew said, 'you have to let go and pray that the children will be OK on their own.'

I could understand what he was saying, but I wondered if the same was true of children, that sometimes you can't control things and sometimes you have to let go. Maybe you even have to let go of your parents. But then I was all muddled in my head and I couldn't make sense of anything, not even where I was or why I was there.

Now that Cody and I have been on watch together again, we've started to talk about what happened. I don't know if anyone else understands how The Wave affected the two of us, because – except for Uncle Dock – they didn't see it, or feel the first power of it crushing us like nuts in a nutcracker.

And I keep thinking about the wave dream I used to have. What seems especially eerie is that the wave in all of those dreams was The Wave – exactly the same: the same height, the same shape. The only difference is that the wave in my dreams was black, and this one was white.

In my dreams, I was always on land, usually playing on a beach. I remember that in one of the dreams, I could see the wave coming in the distance and I started piling up sandbags to make a barrier. I can't get rid of the feeling that the waves of my dreams were all pointing to The Wave that got us on the ocean.

And now I'm having new dreams, worse ones. In

these I am not on land, but on a boat, and the wave is coming and it gets me and it sweeps me far, far away, and when I wake up from the dream, I feel as if I am still floating, far out at sea.

And I keep coming up with lists of things I want to do, hurry, hurry, things to do. I want to learn how to weave – to build my own loom and weave silky cloths like my mother does. I want to go hot-air ballooning. Skydive. Hike the Appalachian Trail. Mountain-bike a thousand miles. Canoe down a long, long river and camp along the way. Climb mountains. Build a cabin on an island like the woman with her dog on Grand Manan.

And I want to take people with me. Bompie and Cody and Uncle Dock. My parents. Even Brian and Uncle Stew could come.

Maybe sailing will go back on my list once we reach Ireland. The dolphins came back today, and they leaped and rolled and made me laugh. It was like an invitation: *Come on, Sophie, have fun in the sea.*

Cody says he thinks that we built up energy on the first part of our trip – getting stronger, storing energy – and when the wave hit, the energy became a protective layer that wrapped itself around us and saved us. It makes as much sense as anything else does these days.

And Cody said, 'You know what? When that wave hit, you know what I thought about, when the water was pouring over me? I thought about Bompie—'

'I did too!' I said. I'd forgotten that, until Cody

mentioned it. 'In the middle of the wave, when I thought I was underwater, I thought about Bompie struggling in the water – in the rivers, in the ocean—'

'Me too! Isn't that strange?' Cody said. 'You know what I said to myself, under all that water? I said, "*Giddy-up, giddy-up!*" '

'I did too. How weird.'

'Maybe we're losing our marbles,' Cody said.

Last night, Cody and I got into this very serious talk about Life. We wondered if maybe people never die, but simply live on and on, leaving other planes behind. When you come near death, you die on one plane – so to everyone you are with, you are dead – but *you* – the *you* in you – doesn't stop existing. Instead, you keep living the same as always and it just seems as if you've had a close call. We wondered if maybe we're not each just one person, but many people existing on millions of different planes, like a line that branches off and branches again and on it goes, but it always has one central trunk.

I was getting a headache from so much thinking, and then Cody said, 'At night on the ocean, a person thinks strange things. Let's not think any more. Let's juggle.'

So we did. We juggled wet socks.

60

Questions

My father's not yelling at me and he keeps asking me if I'm OK. I want to talk to him, but I don't know how to do it or what to say.

What I wonder is this: how come you don't notice the time going by, and you don't think you are changing in any way, but then all of a sudden you realize that what you are thinking today is different from what you thought yesterday and that you are different from what you were yesterday – or last week – or last month?

I feel as if I've been asleep my whole life, and I wish I'd been asking questions like Sophie does, and I wish I knew more things. But even though I feel that, I don't know how to turn into a person who asks questions, who knows more.

And my father – I have seen him just about every day of my life, and all of a sudden he looks like a complete stranger to me. I don't know anything about him. I don't know where he was born or what he does at work or how he got that scar on his forehead.

Everyone is talking about reaching Ireland, but I feel weird, as if we're not really going to get there, or as if I'm not ready to be there. And what will happen with Sophie when we do reach Bompie? Maybe that's part of the reason I don't want to get there. I'm afraid for Sophie.

And I keep wondering how Sophie knows Bompie's stories and if they really are Bompie's stories, and if they are, did he only tell her ones about struggling in the water, and if he did, why did he do that?

And then I remember one of Bompie's stories that was not about water. It was about his father dying. Last night I dreamed that Bompie was telling me that story, and when I woke up I went looking for my dad, and he was lying on a bunk, and I poked him until he woke up.

'Just checking,' I said.

VI

Land

61

Ahoy, Ahoy

Cody and Dock and I were on watch in the wee hours of the morning when Cody shouted, 'There – ahoy!'

I peered into the darkness. 'What? Where?'

'There – see that dark shape thingy?'

We stared at Cody's dark shape thingy, until we realized it was only a low cloud.

A half hour later, Cody called, 'Ahoy!'

'Where?'

'There – lights!'

'You mean those moving lights – those boat lights?'

'Crumbs,' he said.

But then, just before dawn, there it was, a dark shape peeking out behind blue-grey clouds.

'Ahoy, ahoy, ahoy!' Cody shouted. 'Ahoy, see there?'

It was a mountain. Land. Land ho!

'Oh, mountain,' Cody sang, 'oh, beautiful mountain of mine!'

The land, the land, the land! Oh, blessed, blessed land. Oh, sweet, sweet land!

We roused everyone else, and within a few hours we were sailing along the southern coast of Ireland.

It is such a relief to be able to steer by land instead of compass. Oh, land!

Uncle Dock was in fine form. He stood at the rail, reciting part of a poem. He said it's from *The Rime of the Ancient Mariner*:

Oh! dream of joy! is this indeed
The lighthouse top I see?
Is this the hill? is this the kirk?
Is this mine own countree?

When I asked him to repeat it so I could copy it down, he said that the word country is spelled *countree*. I liked that. I had to ask him what a *kirk* was. He said it was a church. Sure enough, from where we stood, we could see both a lighthouse and a church.

So we all recited it again with Uncle Dock, and when we finished, Cody added, 'Oh, Rosalie!'

Uncle Dock said, 'Why'd you say that?'

Cody said, 'I dunno. It just seemed to fit somehow.'

We've come up along the south-west coast, and now we are nearing Crosshaven. The weather is kind and the sun is shining brighter than ever to light up the rocky cliffs and nubby green fields of Ireland. We've passed old castles and farms, cows grazing and tiny cars puttering along. I want to pump up the inflatable dinghy and rush to shore.

But a fight has broken out down below between Uncle Stew and Uncle Mo. Much shouting going on and the sound of things being thrown about.

62

Land

We are on land! We are alive and we are on land!

I thought I was hallucinating when we first spotted land, real earth with trees growing on it and cars rolling along it.

And then we nearly didn't make it into the harbour, because my dad and Uncle Stew got into a major, major fight. It started with Uncle Stew asking who was going to sort out getting *The Wanderer* repaired, and if the rest of us should rent a car and drive on to Bompie's instead of waiting to sail to England when *The Wanderer* was fixed.

In the middle of arguing over that, they started fighting over which adult would stay with the boat, and then Uncle Stew said Sophie should stay too; she shouldn't go to Bompie's! Brian agreed with him. Then Sophie came below deck in the middle of all this and said, 'I'm going to Bompie's and that's that.'

It's a mess.

We tried phoning Mom, but there was no answer. Then Sophie tried her parents: no answer. Then Uncle Stew tried phoning his wife, and he got the answering machine, so he left a message saying we'd arrived. I couldn't believe no one was home! I thought they'd all be waiting by the phone, but Uncle Dock said, 'Well, they had no idea when we'd reach land – it could've been three days ago or next week or—' and he's right, I guess, but it would've been nice to hear a familiar voice celebrating our arrival.

Sophie got a little panicky. 'Where *are* they?' she asked, over and over.

Right now we are wobbling around learning how to walk again, and my dad has gone off to rent a car to drive from here to England, and we still don't know who is going yet.

But we're on land! And we're alive!

63

Bursting

I wasn't going to write in this journal once we reached land, but Cody's still writing in his dog-log. He says the journey isn't over yet.

Yesterday afternoon, once we'd docked *The Wanderer*, we stumbled out onto land, and it was so weird. We looked so silly, wobbling around, as if the land were moving underneath us and we couldn't stay upright. That's the first time I felt seasick – on land!

We went into a pub and ordered up all kinds of food – big plates of it, with things swimming in gravy, and fat loaves of fresh bread and fresh vegetables and fruits. How odd not to have to hold on to our plates as we ate, and how strange to be able to eat and drink at the same time.

We were all chattering away like crazy, talking to anyone who would listen. At one point I looked around, and we were each talking to a different stranger, each of us pouring out our tale.

'You should have seen that storm—'

'Our booms came apart—'

'The waves – like mountains—'

'Knocked out the radar, everything—'

'Thought we were done for—'

'Cracked open my face—'

'The wind – like nothing you can imagine – the sound—'

'Slammed—'

'Blown—'

'Pushed—'

We were bursting. The strangers were nodding at us, tossing out their own stories.

'The sea's a devil—'

'A tricky creature she is—'

'And my uncle, he drowned out there—'

'Seventeen boats lost back in '92—'

'See this leg? Not a real one. The sea, she claimed the real one—'

For hours we went on like that, pouring out the words, and at one point I wondered how much these strangers cared about what we were saying, or if they cared at all, and why we felt such an urgent need to tell them our story, and why they told us theirs.

In the middle of all this, I could sense Cody watching me and listening to what I was saying, as if what I was saying was odd. I tried to listen to what I was saying, but I was so caught up in the telling and in listening to everybody else, that I couldn't concentrate.

As the light faded outside the windows, it felt like we knew these people and they knew us. They told us where to get rooms for the night and followed us down to *The Wanderer*, where they shook their heads over the sorry-looking state of Dock's 'baby', and they helped us lug our wet clothes up the long hill, and bid us all a calm and peaceful night on their own Irish soil.

I dreamed strange dreams, with so many people coming and going in them. There was Dock's friend Joey from Block Island, and Frank and his family from Grand Manan, the lady and her dog, and Dock's Rosalie, and the Irish strangers, and in and out of all these people wandered Cody and Uncle Dock and Stew and Mo and Brian. And me. There were other people too – people who looked familiar, and who seemed to know me, but they faded into the crowd before I could figure out who they were.

64

New Body

It's barely light out but I can't sleep. Everything smells and feels different. No rocking and rolling, no wind. We're in an Irish inn at the top of a hill, and from the window I can see the harbour, and I can just make out *The Wanderer* bobbing there.

Yesterday was so peculiar. I felt like I had a new body and the new body didn't know how to work very well. It was walking funny and knocking into stuff and wanting to touch the strangest things: the floor, the pillows, dry towels.

We were all pretty hyper last night, talking away as if we'd just been given voices. I never heard Sophie talk so much. At first, I was talking so much myself that I wasn't listening to anyone else. And then I heard Brian say, 'I was sleeping when it hit, and I thought I was a goner! I've never been so scared in my whole life! I felt like a little puny chicken in a meat market.' He was thumping on the table and clutching at his throat, and I don't know, he just surprised me because he could make that whole scary thing into something that was almost funny.

And then I heard Sophie tell someone, 'Yep, these are my cousins' – and she pointed to me and Brian – 'and we've been planning this trip since we were little kids—'

I was going to correct her, and then I realized she was

mixing her story with my dad's and Uncle Stew's and Uncle Dock's.

'Brian didn't think we'd really do it,' she said, 'but I always knew we'd do it.'

And then she was talking about The Wave, and how it rose up behind the boat. 'And it was so black and tall and—'

The Wave was white.

65

Push–Pull

We're in the car on the way to Bompie's: me, Cody, Brian, Uncle Mo, Uncle Stew and Uncle Dock. Uncle Dock found someone to start repair work on *The Wanderer* while we all drive on to Bompie's. This was after a huge fight. Now, everyone's touchy and crabby and hardly speaking. Uncle Dock is really disappointed that we can't sail *The Wanderer* around the Irish coast because he wanted to stop at a friend's house in one of the coastal towns. Finally, he got the other uncles to agree that we could drive that way and stop there briefly.

'But we're not staying!' Uncle Stew said.

'We're not spending a week there or anything,' Uncle Mo said.

We couldn't get the phones in the inn to work last night, so we still haven't called home. It makes me jittery. Where is everyone? I hope we can call from Uncle Dock's friend's house.

We're crammed in like sardines in this car and it's hard to write because Brian keeps looking over my shoulder, trying to see what I'm writing. Uncle Stew is driving and we'll be lucky to get there alive. We're careening around narrow roads and he keeps forgetting to drive on the left side. We've already nearly wiped out a flock of sheep and a couple of farmers.

Everything is so beautiful: green, green land and cliffs overlooking the sea. Were we really tossing about on that sea just a few days ago? I wish everyone wasn't in such a bad mood so that we could stop and wander through some of these little towns, but the uncles look mighty determined. They have their sights set now on a quick stop at Uncle Dock's friend's and then getting on to Bompie.

I'm feeling pushed and pulled: I long to see Bompie, but I'm also terrified of seeing Bompie.

66

The Visitor

Wonder of wonder of wonders!

We squeezed down a narrow lane in a tiny village along the Irish coast, and we pulled up outside a wee cottage, and Uncle Dock went up to the door, and when it opened, he staggered back and clutched his chest.

We were all sticking our heads out the windows like a bunch of goons, trying to get a better look. Then Uncle Dock was hugging the life out of someone in a yellow dress, and we heard him say, 'Oh! Rosalie!'

'Rosalie?' we all said. 'Rosalie?'

And then we were pouring out of the car, and Uncle Dock let go of Rosalie so we could take a good look at her. She has the sweetest face you ever saw and very big round eyes, and she was smiling the biggest smile you ever saw, except maybe for Uncle Dock's smile, which was the biggest smile in the universe.

67

Phone Calls

This weird life we're in is getting weirder and weirder. Yesterday, Uncle Dock got the surprise of his life when he found Rosalie at his – and her – friend's house in Ireland. I didn't think we were ever going to tear the two of them apart.

Dock's friend let us use the phone, so we all called home and everybody was jumping up and down on both sides of the ocean, and people were shouting and laughing, and then we all flopped down on the floor in a used-up heap.

Sophie kept saying, 'I can't believe it. I didn't ever think I was going to hear their voices again. I'm not dreaming, right? I called and they were there, right?'

The only not-so-good news in the day was that Sophie's mother said Bompie hadn't been well, and that if we hadn't called her by tomorrow to say that we were nearly to Bompie, she was going to get on a plane and go see him herself.

So then we were all rushing around, hurrying to get on to Bompie's, and Dock didn't want to leave Rosalie, and we practically had to pull him out the door. The only reason Dock left at all is that Rosalie promised to join him at Bompie's in a couple of days.

As soon as we were all back in the car, everyone started saying, 'Rosalie! Oh, Rosalie!' and Uncle Dock was blushing, but he was so happy he didn't even mind us teasing him.

*

Now we're on the ferry, steaming across the Irish Sea towards Wales. I keep looking for the sails, feeling as if I'm supposed to be doing something. None of us were too eager to get back on a boat, I can tell you that.

'Isn't there a bridge?' my father kept asking. 'Are you sure there isn't a bridge over to Wales?'

'Doofus,' Uncle Stew said.

'Don't start up with me,' my father warned.

Brian keeps bugging Sophie. He said, 'So, you think Bompie will recognize – us?'

'Of course he'll recognize us,' Sophie said.

'All of us?'

'Of course,' Sophie said.

But there's something different in the way Brian is bugging Sophie now. It doesn't seem as mean as before; it's more like he is trying very hard to figure her out and he's worried about her too. He likes truth and facts and lists, and I think he is very bothered by someone like Sophie who sees the world differently than he does. Brian keeps asking me what is going on with Sophie and what's going to happen once we reach Bompie's. I told him I wasn't a mind-reader or a fortune-teller.

68

Wales

Down and across Wales we've plunged. The countryside is so green and lush and inviting, but it's so hard to get used to the cars and noise and speed. I wish we would stop more. I long to look in the windows of the houses and listen to the people talk. What do they do every day? Who is living in all those houses?

But we're pressing on to Bompie's because Bompie hasn't been well and everyone is worried now, and it all scares me half to death. Before I was just scared about seeing Bompie and what that would mean, but now I'm afraid he won't even be alive when we get there, and that would be much, much worse.

We've stopped now at a little inn in a dark, quiet village and I'm going back downstairs now to listen to the people talk.

69

The Little Girl

We've zoomed across Wales. Boy, did Sophie love Wales! She kept saying, 'Wouldn't you like to live here? In this village? Where would we go to school? What would we eat for breakfast? Who do you think lives in that little house there?'

But last night was the strangest of all. We were at an inn, waiting downstairs for Sophie so we could have dinner, and Brian was badgering Uncle Dock to tell us what had happened to Sophie's real parents.

'We have a right to know,' Brian insisted.

'I don't know about that,' Uncle Dock said.

'What happened?' Uncle Stew said. 'Nobody ever tells me anything.'

Brian said, 'Why is she always lying about her parents? Those aren't her parents. Why is she lying about Bompie? I'm going to ask her straight out why she's lying.'

'Sophie's not lying,' Uncle Dock said.

'Is too,' Brian said.

Uncle Dock said, 'Look, I tell you what. I'll tell you a story—'

'I don't want a story,' Brian said. 'I want the truth.'

'Just listen,' Uncle Dock said. 'Once there was a child who lived with her parents by the ocean. They were a nice little family and the girl was much loved. But something happened – the parents – the parents died, and then—'

My head felt like it was being bombarded by a whole cloud of zinging fireworks. 'Wait!' I said. 'So afterwards, everyone was telling the little girl how the parents went to heaven—'

'Well, I don't know exactly—' Dock said.

I kept going. 'Everyone was saying how heaven was such a beautiful place and all, with no worries, no woes, and that made the little girl feel awful, that she was left behind while the parents were off in this beautiful place without her—'

'Well, erm, I don't know exactly,' Dock said. 'I just know that then the little girl went to live with—'

'Wait,' I said. 'Her grandfather? Did she live with her grandfather?'

'Yep,' Uncle Dock said. 'But she only lived with her grandfather for a short time, and when he died, she went to an aunt's house, but the aunt—'

'The aunt didn't want the little girl, right?' I said. 'And so the girl went to a foster home or something and then another and another. Nobody wanted her probably. She lived in a lot, a lot of places, right?'

'Yep,' Uncle Dock said.

'What the heck is going on?' Brian said. 'How do you know this stuff, Cody?'

'How come nobody ever tells me this stuff?' Uncle Stew said.

'So,' I said, 'the little girl finally, finally was adopted, right?'

'Yep,' Uncle Dock said.

'And by this time,' – I was really talking fast now – 'by this time, she wanted so much to be wanted that she made herself believe that this was her real family, her only family, and they had chosen her and they loved her and they couldn't live without her.'

When I got to that point, Sophie came into the room, and we all stared at her, and Brian put his head in his hands and said, 'Oh. Oh!' and Uncle Stew said, 'Oh Lord. Nobody ever tells me a darn thing!'

And then we had dinner.

I could hardly eat because all I could do was look at Sophie, this whole new Sophie, and everybody else was looking at her too, and finally she put her fork down and said, 'Exactly why is everyone staring at me like I'm a ghost or something?'

Uncle Dock said, 'You just look real special tonight, Sophie, that's all,' and she bent her head, and I watched one lone tear drop down her cheek and onto her plate.

We've just crossed the Severn River (there was a bridge! no ferry!) and are now in England. Both Uncle Dock and my father cried when we entered England. Sophie asked them what was the matter and Uncle Dock said, 'England! England!' which wasn't exactly an answer.

Sophie said, 'What about England?'

My dad said, 'Our father was born here.'

'I know,' Sophie said.

'So why does that make you cry?' Brian asked.

'Our father. Bompie. Born here.' My dad turned to Uncle Stew. 'You know what I mean? Bompie was born here.'

Uncle Stew, who was driving, said, 'I have to concentrate here – where do we go now? Who has the map?'

My dad turned to Uncle Dock. 'Dock? You explain. It's a little emotional—'

'Sure,' Dock said. 'I know what you mean. Our own father was born in this very country, and it's like part of us is here too. We came out of all this—'

And then they were all very quiet, staring out at the countryside.

'Just think,' Sophie said. 'If Bompie and his parents hadn't come to America, you would have grown up in England too. You wouldn't be Americans. This would be your home.'

My dad nodded. 'That's exactly what I was thinking.'

Brian said, 'Well, if Bompie had grown up here, maybe he wouldn't have married who he married and you all wouldn't be here. Or maybe if you *were* here, you'd all have grown up here and you wouldn't have married who you married and then I wouldn't be here. Or Cody—'

Sophie whispered, 'Would I be here?'

And everyone looked at her and then back out at the countryside and Brian said, very soberly, 'Now that is the question of the century.'

Sophie leaned her head against the window and closed her eyes. I think she's sleeping now.

Brian just whispered to me, 'But what about the Bompie stories? How does she know the Bompie stories? Did she make them up?'

'I don't know,' I said. And now I'm thinking about all the other things I don't know about Sophie. I want to know *how* her parents died. Did they get a terrible disease? Did they die at the same time or did they die one at a time, and if they did, which one died first? And what did Sophie think? And how did Sophie feel?

I wonder what Sophie is dreaming.

We'll be at Bompie's tonight.

70

The Castle

Across England we've come: past Bristol and Swindon and Reading, and now we're sitting on a bench outside Windsor Castle, which looms up behind us, a great grey stone castle. Inside, the Queen is probably having tea. Across the street is McDonald's. We're eating cheeseburgers, right here outside Windsor Castle.

The air is warm and heavy with anticipation. We are very close to Bompie's, maybe a half hour away.

I guess we are going. Now.

71

The Cottage

When I woke up this morning, I thought maybe I had landed on another planet and I was in someone else's body. This was partly because I had slept the night on the floor and partly because of what greeted us when we got to Bompie's last night.

We found the village of Thorpe without too much trouble, but since the houses don't have numbers, finding Bompie's house in the dark was a little harder. The houses all have names, like Glenacre and The Yellow Cottage and The Green Cottage and The Old Post Office.

The name of Bompie's house is Walnut Tree Cottage, so we spent a lot of time peering out at trees, looking for a walnut tree, and as it turned out there is no longer a walnut tree at Bompie's house anyway. The way we finally found it was by stopping at a house and when I went up and knocked on the door, a woman answered and said, 'You'll be wanting that one across the way, love,' and she pointed to a little white cottage across the street.

All the lights were on in Bompie's cottage. We tapped on the door, and when it opened, a nurse answered. Uncle Dock explained who we were and then we all squeezed inside, and Uncle Dock said, 'Where is he?'

She led us through one room and then another, where the ceilings are so low you bump your head, and we followed her on through another room and down a skinny hallway and into Bompie's bedroom.

And there was Bompie, lying in his bed with his eyes closed. I was pretty sure our luck had run out and he was dead.

72

Bompie

Oh, Bompie!

I can see why he wanted to come home to his England. It's so pretty here, with roses climbing up the side of the house, and lavender spreading in big clumps along the walk, and inside are tiny rooms and wee windows and miniature fireplaces.

I had so wanted to see him alone, but instead we all clumped into the room together.

'Is he dead?' Cody asked.

'Shh,' the nurse said. 'No, he's not dead, but he's a little confused. Don't scare him.'

He looked different than I expected him to look, but I figured that was because his eyes and mouth were closed. What I saw was a gentle round face, very pale, with wisps of grey hair over the top of his head. He looked like an older version of Uncle Dock.

Uncle Dock took Bompie's hand and stroked it gently. 'Bompie,' he whispered. 'Bompie?'

Bompie opened his eyes, blinked and stared. 'Peter?' he said to Uncle Dock.

'Peter?' Uncle Dock said. 'Who's Peter? It's me – Dock – Jonah.'

'Jonah is away,' Bompie said. 'He's at camp.'

Uncle Dock bit his lip.

'Bompie?' Uncle Mo said.

Bompie stared hard at Uncle Mo. 'Who are you?' he asked.

'It's me, Moses.'

'Moses is away,' Bompie said. 'He's at camp.'

Uncle Stew said, 'Bompie? Do you know me? It's Stuart.'

Bompie blinked again, three or four times. 'Stuart is away,' he said. 'He's at camp.'

And then Cody stepped forward and Bompie said, 'Oh! There's Moses. Are you back from camp?'

Cody said, 'Yes. I'm back from camp.'

And when Brian stepped forward, Bompie said, 'And here's Stuart! You've come back from camp too?'

And Brian said, 'Yes.'

And then I stepped forward and I knelt beside Bompie, and I said, 'Bompie? Do you know who I am?'

And he stared hard at me and said, 'Are you Margaret?'

I said, 'No.'

'Claire?'

'No.'

Brian said, 'Sophie, stop. He doesn't know you.'

And Bompie said, 'Sophie! Are you Sophie?'

And I said, 'Yes.'

73

The Story

It seems way more than a week ago that we arrived here at Bompie's, and it seems a lifetime ago that we set sail on our first ocean shakedown.

For the first day we were here, Bompie slept most of the time and didn't recognize us. On the second day, Sophie started telling Bompie his own stories. She said, 'Remember, Bompie, when you were young and living on the farm in Kentucky, and your family traded two mules for a car? Remember that, Bompie?'

He opened his eyes very wide and nodded.

'And remember, Bompie, how you went to town to pick up the car and drive it home? And on the way home—'

With each detail, Bompie nodded and said, 'Yes, yes, that was me.'

'And in the water, when you were struggling, struggling—'

'Me?' Bompie said.

'All that water, and you were underneath—'

'That part I don't remember so good,' Bompie said.

That afternoon, Sophie told another story to him. 'Remember, Bompie, when you were young and living in Kentucky, near the Ohio River, and one day you started across the train bridge—'

'The trestle, yes, yes,' Bompie said.

'And remember how it was so windy and rainy—'

'Yes, yes.'

'And when the train came, you had to let go and you fell down into the water—'

'Yes, yes, that was me.'

'And all that swirling water turning you this way and that and you were fighting for breath and—'

'That part I don't remember so good,' Bompie said.

She told Bompie all the stories she'd told us, and we all wandered in and out of the room as she was doing this, and everyone else was very quiet, listening. Bompie remembered almost everything she described, except for the parts about struggling in the water.

Once, when I was in there with Sophie, she told a story I hadn't heard her tell before. It went like this:

'Bompie, remember when you were very little, just a child, and you went sailing with your parents?'

'I did?' he said.

'Out on the ocean, the wide blue blue ocean. And you were sailing, sailing along, and then the sky got very grey and the wind started to howl – remember?'

He looked at her, blinked a few times, but said nothing.

'The wind, remember? It was howling howling howling, and the boat was rolling, and it got so cold, and your mother wrapped you in a blanket and put you in the dinghy – remember?'

Bompie stared at her, but still he said nothing. Sophie rushed on, 'Remember? Remember? And – and – the wind – the cold – and water, a big wall of black water coming down over you and then you were floating floating floating – and – and – the parents – the parents—'

She looked at me, pleading, and suddenly so much was so clear to me. I knelt on the other side of the bed. 'The parents didn't make it,' I said.

Sophie gasped. 'The parents didn't make it,' she repeated, and then she rushed on, 'And then you were all alone, Bompie, all by yourself, floating floating—'

Bompie said, 'But I—'

I reached across the bed and touched her hand. 'Sophie,' I said. 'Maybe that's not Bompie's story. Maybe that's your story.'

Bompie whispered, 'Sophie, he's right. That's your story, honey.'

Sophie stared at me and then at Bompie. She looked so scared and so little sitting there beside Bompie. And then she put her head down on Bompie's chest and she cried and cried and cried.

I left them there together and went out into the backyard and lay down in the grass beneath the apple tree.

About an hour later, Sophie came out and handed me a blue cloth-covered notebook.

'I want you to read this,' she whispered. 'He's your Bompie too,' and then she walked through the gate and down the village lane.

In the notebook were handwritten letters, maybe twenty or thirty of them, dated over the past three years. They were all addressed 'To my Sophie,' and they were all signed, 'From your Bompie.'

The first one was welcoming her to the family. He told her that he could be her grandpa; he would be her Bompie.

In each of the other letters he told her a story about himself growing up, so that she would know him better, he said.

There were many more stories besides the ones Sophie had already told us. There were stories about him in school and about him fishing with his own grandfather; there were stories about the first girl he had kissed and about the day he met Margaret, his wife.

It was strange reading the ones about the car in the river, and leaping off the train tracks, and Bompie's baptism, and Bompie in the swimming hole, and Bompie at the ocean. Most of what Sophie had told us was pretty much the way he had told it to her in his letters, except for the parts about struggling in the water. He was in the water all those times, but he hadn't written about struggling in it.

Those parts had come from Sophie.

When I finished reading, I walked up and down the village lanes, looking for Sophie.

74

Apples

Bompie's yard looks so pretty: roses and lavender and delphiniums and petunias and pansies. In the backyard is an apple tree, full of nearly ripe apples. On our third day here, Uncle Mo went out and picked some of the ripest, and later that day he walked into Bompie's bedroom and said, 'Bompie? Look what I brought you—'

Bompie sat up and said, 'Apple pie!' and he laughed and then he cried and then he laughed again, and Uncle Mo was laughing and crying too, and then everyone came in the room and we were all laughing and crying over that apple pie.

'How'd you know how to make that?' Uncle Stew said.

'Found Grandma's cookbook! Followed the recipe!' Uncle Mo was very proud of himself. 'I'm not a complete doofus!'

That afternoon, when Cody and I were sitting with Bompie, watching him sleep, Bompie took a short, quick breath, and then another, and then there was a long pause before another breath, and then it was quiet.

Cody and I stared at each other. Then Bompie

spluttered and took another breath and went on breathing.

'Were you thinking what I was thinking?' Cody asked. 'Were you thinking, *Giddy-up, Bompie*?'

'Yes, I was,' I said.

You would think that at a time like that, with Bompie frail in his bed, everyone would be extra kind and quiet and considerate, but Uncle Stew and Uncle Mo got into one of their big arguments. It was over whether or not they should take Bompie back to America.

'How can he stay here?' Uncle Stew demanded. 'He can't take care of himself – who will look after him? I say he comes back to America.'

'I say he stays here,' Uncle Mo said. 'And besides, if he comes to America, where will he live? Will you take him?'

Uncle Stew spluttered. 'Me? We don't have room – we aren't set up for – why don't you take him?'

Uncle Dock intervened. 'Maybe you should ask Bompie what he wants to do.'

And so they asked Bompie, and he said, 'I'm home! I'm staying put!' Uncle Dock said that Bompie had made his choice. He had come home, and it was a beautiful place, and we ought to let him stay in his England, with the roses and the lavender growing all around.

'So who's going to take care of him?' Uncle Stew asked.

'I could,' I said. 'For the summer. Couldn't I?'

'Too young,' Uncle Stew said. Then he crossed his arms over his chest, the way Brian does sometimes, and said, 'You know what? I am not going to worry about this. You all worry about it. I'm going to take a nap.'

About that time, Rosalie arrived, and so we all stood around gawking at Dock and Rosalie. They must've gotten tired of us staring at them, though, because pretty soon they said they were going out for a walk.

In the kitchen, Brian was copying the apple pie recipe. 'I've been thinking about that pie all the way across the ocean,' he said. 'I'm going to learn how to make it too.'

'Hey,' Cody said. 'Look out there—'

Out in the backyard, Uncle Mo was juggling apples. He kept on juggling even when we went out to watch. 'Look at this,' he said. 'I can do four at a time! This is pretty cool, this juggling. What do you think, Sierra-Oscar-November?'

'Pretty cool, Delta-Alpha-Delta,' Cody said, 'pretty cool.'

So the rest of us started picking apples and we went over to Bompie's window, where he was propped up on pillows watching us, and we all started juggling, and we were clunking each other over the head a lot with flying apples, and that's where Uncle Dock found us when he came back from his walk.

75

Oh, Rosalie!

Women!

Rosalie's gone.

Uncle Dock came back from his walk alone and looking grim. We pounded him with questions, wanting to know where Rosalie was.

'Gone,' he said.

'Gone?' Sophie said. 'She can't be gone. She just got here—'

'Gone,' Uncle Dock repeated. 'Gone, gone, gone.'

Then everyone was asking questions a mile a minute, wanting to know where she went and why she went and if she was coming back.

Uncle Dock said, 'She had some plans she couldn't change. She's leaving tomorrow for Spain.'

Then Sophie said, 'Go get her!' and Brian said, 'Stop her!'

Uncle Dock shrugged. 'She's got a mind of her own, that Rosalie.'

Brian and Sophie kept saying 'Go get her!' and then, I don't know where this came from, but I said, 'Why didn't you ask her to marry you or something?'

'I did,' Uncle Dock said.

'Way to go, Dock,' Uncle Mo said.

I said, 'So what did she say? Why did she go?'

'Like I said, she has some plans.'

'But what did she say about the getting married part?' I asked.

Uncle Dock stood there tossing a lone green apple up and down with one hand. 'She said it was too soon—'

'Too *soon*?' Sophie said. 'You've been waiting your whole life. You've been pining away—'

'Shoot,' Uncle Dock said. 'Can't a guy have any secrets around here?'

Then somebody said maybe Rosalie would change her mind or maybe she would go finish her plans and come back, and then Sophie said, 'If you two ever do get married, you're not going to make her do all the housework and stuff, are you?'

Uncle Stew, who had joined us by then, said, 'OK, enough of this chatter. What are we going to do about the looking-after-Bompie question?'

'I may have solved that one,' Uncle Dock said.

'How?' Uncle Stew said.

'I'm going to stay here,' Uncle Dock said. 'I'll stay here in England. I'll look after him.'

Everyone else seemed relieved and seemed to think it was a good solution. Later, though, when Brian and Sophie and I were packing up our things, Brian said, 'I think it's sad. Uncle Dock just found Rosalie, and then he loses her again. And now he's going to give up everything and stay here to take care of an old man.'

I told him that Bompie wasn't just an old man, that he was Uncle Dock's *father*.

And then Sophie started wondering if maybe Rosalie would change her mind someday, and if Bompie might get better, and then I said maybe we could visit them in England, like in the summers, and then Sophie said, 'And maybe we could all take another trip on *The Wanderer*.'

'Cool,' I said. 'We'll all take a trip and we'll sail really far—'

'Not *too* far,' Brian said. 'Not *too* soon.'

And Sophie said that if Rosalie wasn't back by then, we could all go searching for Rosalie, oh, Rosalie!

76

Gifts

Last night we all sat around with Bompie, and we told him about our trip over on *The Wanderer*, and he seemed absorbed in all of it. When we finished, Bompie said, 'You all are the ones who should be eating the pie. Where's the pie? More pie!'

Uncle Mo said, 'Wait a minute – I've got something—'

We thought he was going to bring in some pie, but instead he brought in a bunch of flat packages. He lifted one off the top and said, 'This one's for Bompie.'

Bompie tore the paper off the package, and inside was one of Mo's drawings. It was a sketch of Bompie sitting up in bed, eating pie.

'Pie!' Bompie said. 'Ha, ha, ha! Pie!'

At the bottom of the drawing, Uncle Mo had written *Ulysses Eating Pie*.

'Ulysses!' Bompie said. 'Ha, ha, ha! That's *me*!'

Uncle Mo passed out packages to Uncle Stew and Brian and Uncle Dock. The one for Uncle Stew was a drawing of Stew and Brian using the sextant. The one for Brian was a sketch of Brian tacking up a list in the galley. The one for Uncle Dock was a watercolour of Dock's 'baby', *The Wanderer*, with Captain Dock at the bow.

We were all ooh-ing and aah-ing over these drawings.

'Now, this one's for Cody,' Uncle Mo said.

Cody ripped off the wrapping. Inside was a pen-and-ink drawing of Cody juggling. He was standing on *The Wanderer*, and the boat was leaning way over, but Cody was perfectly balanced, and he was juggling not pretzels – or socks – but people. Each of us was a little wee tiny person up in the air, and Cody was juggling us.

'Man!' Cody said. 'This is amazing!'

'Did you notice the knots?' Uncle Mo said.

We all looked closer. And then we saw them. Cody's hair was all tied up in little end-knots and clove hitches.

'This is the most brilliant drawing I ever saw in my whole life,' Cody said.

I think Uncle Mo was pleased by that compliment.

Then Cody said, 'Wait!' and he dashed out of the room, and when he came back, he handed Uncle Mo a page that he'd torn from his dog-log. 'For you,' he said. 'I'll clean up the edges—'

'For me?' Uncle Mo said.

It was a drawing of Uncle Mo, leaning back in a deckchair on *The Wanderer*. In his lap was his sketchbook. Underneath, Cody had written *Moses, The Artist.*

'*Moses,*' Uncle Mo said. 'That's *me*!'

Bompie said, 'Hey! What about those other two thingys over there? Who are those for?'

Uncle Mo said, 'Oh. Right. These last two were supposed to be for the newest members of the family, but—' He looked at Uncle Dock. 'This one was supposed to be for Rosalie. I guess you should open it—'

Uncle Dock slowly unwrapped it. Inside was a drawing of three whales: the mother and the baby and father whales that we had seen on the ocean.

'Oh,' Uncle Dock whispered. 'Oh, Rosalie—'

Bompie said, 'Rosalie? Who's this Rosalie everyone keeps talking about? Do I know Rosalie?'

Cody said, 'She's this really neat woman that Uncle Dock knows. She's temporarily lost.'

'Send out a search party!' Bompie said.

We all looked at Uncle Dock. 'I get the hint,' he said. 'Now what about that last package?'

Uncle Mo said, 'This one's for Sophie.'

My fingers were trembling. A present? For me? I could hardly get the wrapping off, I was so excited. Inside was one of Mo's drawings.

There I was, swinging high up in the air in the bosun's chair, swinging way out over the waves, and the water was very blue, and the sky was blue, and beneath me, in the blue water, was a pair of dolphins, leaping in the air.

Underneath the drawing, Uncle Mo had written, *Giddy-up, Sophie!*

77

Remembering

It sure was hard saying goodbye to Uncle Dock and to Bompie. But we did, and we flew over that wide, wide ocean, and it was amazing to realize we'd sailed all the way across it.

I'm home, and Sophie is staying here for the week. We went down to the oceanside yesterday and walked along the beach and stared out at the water and we couldn't stop talking about our trip. We went all the way back to when we'd first seen *The Wanderer* and all the things we'd fixed on her, and we remembered going to Block Island and Martha's Vineyard and Grand Manan, and then that long, scary stretch across to Ireland.

I said, 'You know when you said you went clamming on Block Island with Bompie when you were little?'

'Yeah,' she said.

'If you don't want to remember this, that's OK, but I was wondering, maybe that was your other Bompie, your first Bompie—'

She stopped right in her tracks. 'My first Bompie?'

'Yeah, maybe that's who took you clamming, and maybe you were with your parents too – your first parents—'

'My first parents?'

'That sounded like a really nice time,' I said. 'That would be a good thing to remember, wouldn't it? That little kid you told me about – that little kid wouldn't mind remembering things like that, would she?'

'That little kid is bigger now,' she said.

I've been thinking about the little kid. I think that one day the little kid got lucky and she landed in a place where it was OK if she couldn't remember all the time, and because it was OK *not* to remember, she started to remember. And along with the painful things came the good things to remember and maybe she felt as if she'd found some things she'd lost.

Uncle Stew phoned to say he'd found a job with a company that charts the ocean bottom. 'You should see the equipment they have!' he said. 'It'll be cool to see what's down there at the bottom of the ocean.'

At first Sophie was really intrigued by that and was asking a million questions about what kind of equipment and what sort of stuff it could find, but later she said she wasn't so sure she wanted to know what was on the bottom of the ocean.

And my dad has enrolled in art classes at night. 'Does that mean you get to do what you want to do?' Sophie asked him.

My dad said, 'Well, during the day I'll still crunch numbers, but at night – at night I'll be Moses the Artist.'

Uncle Dock phoned to say that *The Wanderer* was fixed and that he thought Bompie might be well enough by next month to take a little sail with him.

Sophie said, 'Don't let him fall overboard. Don't let him fall in that water.'

I said, 'Maybe you could sail over to Spain.'

Uncle Dock said, 'Yep, you just never know where we might end up.'

Next week, Sierra-Oscar-Papa-Hotel-India-Echo and Bravo-Romeo-India-Alpha-November and I are going to meet up at Sophie's to check out the Ohio River. Sophie says a raft on the river will seem real calm after that ocean. Brian's busy making out lists of what we will need in order to build the raft, and we've already decided to paint the raft blue and name it *The Blue Bopper Wanderer*.

'We'll find that bridge Bompie jumped off of,' I said.

'And the place where Bompie and the car turned over in the river,' Brian said.

'And where Bompie got baptized and bit the pastor,' Sophie said.

I guess this dog-log is over, though.

Bravo-Yankee-Echo-Bravo-Yankee-Echo.

78

Home

I'm home, and it sure is nice to be home. Cody and Brian are here for a couple of weeks too.

I can tell that my now-parents are awfully relieved that I made it back in one piece. They keep coming into my room at night and sitting on the edge of my bed, and when I open my eyes, they say, 'You OK? You need anything?' and I say, 'I'm just fine.'

On the first night home, my dad made barbecued chicken and corn on the cob, my favourites.

Cody said, 'Yum, beauteous chicken!'

Brian said, 'Yum, beauteous corn on the cob!'

For dessert we had great big chocolate fudge sundaes. Brian said, 'Guess we're going to have to show them how to make pie.'

Yesterday, Cody and Brian and I were standing by the Ohio River, watching the current carry branches and leaves down under the train bridge and along, beyond it, round the bend.

'Don't you wonder what's around that bend?' Cody asked.

'You been there, Sophie?' Brian asked.

'Nope,' I said. 'Not yet.'

'Well?' Cody said. 'What do you think? Want

to cast off the flibbergibbet on *The Blue Bopper Wanderer* and go that way?'

'Soon as we get some wooden paddle thingys,' I said.

Brian said, 'Huh, huh, huh, huh, huh, huh.'

I'm not in dreamland or earthland or mule-land. I'm just right here, right now. When I close my eyes, I can still smell the sea, but I feel as if I've been dunked in the clear cool water and I've come out all clean and new.

Bye-bye, Bompie. Bye-bye, sea.

Sharon Creech

Walk Two Moons

Just over a year ago, my father plucked me up like a weed and took me and all our belongings (no, that is not true – he did not bring the chestnut tree or the willow or the maple or the hayloft or the swimming hole or any of those things which belong to me) and we drove three hundred miles straight north and stopped in front of a house in Euclid, Ohio.

There, Salamanca Hiddle begins to unravel the mystery that surrounds her world – a world from which her mother has suddenly, and without warning, disappeared.

'A powerful, emotional narrative which keeps the reader guessing right up to the end.'
Smarties Prize Judges

'A really satisfying book – funny, poignant, cunning in the unravelling of its mysteries . . . A super read.'
Observer

Winner of the Newbery Medal
Winner of the Children's Book Award (Longer Novels)
Shortlisted for the Smarties Book Prize
Winner of the W H Smith Mind Boggling Books Award

Sharon Creech

Absolutely Normal Chaos

So. Here it is. My summer journal. As you can see, I got a little carried away.

The problem is this, though. I don't want you to read it.

I really mean it. I just wanted you to know I did it. I didn't want you to think I was one of those kids who says, 'Oh yeah, I did it, but I lost it/my dog ate it/my little brother dropped it in the toilet.'

But please, PLEEEASE DON'T READ IT! How was I to know all this stuff was going to happen this summer? Sigh.

PLEASE DON'T READ IT. I mean it.

Sincerely,

Mary Lou Finney

Would you want *your* teacher to read your summer diary?

'A stonkingly good read.' *Just Seventeen*

'It's a great book, very difficult to put down once you've started. I loved reading it and I'm sure you will too.' *The Mail*